To resist him was totally beyond Alison's power.

With a shuddering gasp she wound her arms around Rod's neck and kissed him back, with all the fervour and longing of a passionate nature held too long in check. Only when he began to unbutton her top did she finally come to her senses.

'No!' she cried. 'I didn't mean... I swore I'd never... Don't you understand? That's why I came here, so I could be left alone for the rest of my life!'

Angela Devine grew up in Tasmania surrounded by forests, mountains and wild seas, so she dislikes big cities. Before taking up writing, she worked as a teacher, librarian and university lecturer. As a young mother and Ph.D. student, she read romantic fiction for fun and later decided it would be even more fun to write it. She is married with four children, loves chocolate and Twinings teas and hates ironing. Her current hobbies are gardening, bushwalking, travelling and classical music.

Recent titles by the same author:

DARK PIRATE
MISTRESS FOR HIRE

THE PERFECT MAN

BY
ANGELA DEVINE

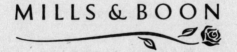

To Lucy with love.

MILLS & BOON and the Rose Device
are trademarks of the publisher.
Harlequin Mills & Boon Limited,
Eton House, 18–24 Paradise Road, Richmond, Surrey TW9 1SR

© Angela Devine 1996

ISBN 0 263 79523 3

Set in 10 on 11½ pt Linotron Times
01-9606-56372

Typeset in Great Britain by CentraCet, Cambridge
Made and printed in Great Britain

CHAPTER ONE

ALL day long Alison had been gripped by an unfamiliar restlessness. The tiny cabin seemed stifling and claustrophobic without her daughter's presence, and in the end she decided to go for a drive. That should calm her down, and settle this mysterious ache of desire for something she couldn't define. Or so she thought. But of course she had no idea of what was about to happen.

She drove for at least twenty minutes, until she was hypnotised by the roar of the surf and the whine of the vehicle's engine. At last she stopped, smack in the middle of a two-hundred-metre wide stretch of sand, turned off the ignition and walked down to the water's edge. The jade-green waves were breaking in long, white frills of surf and the incoming tide was beginning to eat up the great, glassy silver mirror of shallow water along the sea's edge.

At first the sand was as fine and white as ground almonds, then as she walked further it changed to a porridge-like consistency in the shallows. Finally, when she waded out up to her knees, she felt it churn and suck beneath her toes with the boiling force of the current. The clean, scouring salt wind sent her long red-gold hair flapping in streamers behind her, and its roaring filled the air along with the crashing counterpoint of surf.

Alison took in a deep breath and let out a long sigh as her pale blue beach trousers and T-shirt fluttered against her small, compact frame. Even after living here for five years, she never tired of this magnificent, empty expanse of Queensland beach, which stretched for almost forty miles with scarcely a sign of human habitation. All the same, she hadn't been able to fight down a twinge of disappointment when Cathy had refused to come birdwatching with her today.

This was the first time Cathy had ever refused point-blank to accompany her mother. It was meant to be a treat—birdwatching, beachcombing and then camping out, but Cathy had wrinkled her freckled nose in disgust. Alison could almost hear the pert six-year-old's voice echoing in her head.

'Birdwatching's too boring and too lonely! Anyway, Auntie Lyn said she's going to take me into Noosa and buy me party shoes with gold buckles on them.'

Alison smiled wryly. She could hardly blame her daughter for preferring party shoes to pied oyster catchers, but that was no reason why Alison herself shouldn't do some birdwatching. Otherwise what was the point of having four days' break from running tours? Lately business had been so profitable that her brother had hired an extra driver, to give them more time off. That was great for Jerry and his wife, but Alison was finding it more of a burden than a pleasure.

Raising her binoculars, which hung on a leather strap around her neck, she lifted them to her eyes and began to scan the coastline. Immediately the great cliffs of coloured sand leapt into focus, their ridges sculpted by the wind into strange fluted shapes. Then she panned steadily across the beach, pausing for a moment to examine a piece of jagged black driftwood and a yellow and black sea snake cast up by the waves.

Suddenly she saw a flock of terns, grey with white underbellies, rising into the air, wheeling and fluttering like a *corps de ballet*. There must be another vehicle coming! As she watched she saw its dim shape looming up through a flying mist of sand. It was travelling far too fast. Those white expanses of dry sand were terribly deceptive: they looked smooth, but often contained large, dangerous depressions that you couldn't see until you hit them. If only she could warn—

'No!' she cried in horror.

For at that very moment the oncoming vehicle breasted a slight rise in the sand and hit the gully beyond before her very eyes. It shot into the air, spun sideways and struck the sea with a violent smack, sending up a cloud of white spray.

Alison's heart was hammering furiously as she dropped the binoculars, splashed through the foaming shallows and sprinted up the beach. What would she find when she got there? Would the occupants be drowned or have head injuries? Would she be able to save them? There was nobody else to help them. Oh, she must hurry, hurry!

Her fingers shook as she turned the key in the ignition and gunned the engine into life. The vehicle roared into action and she drove as fast as she dared, not wanting to risk an accident herself. Trying to keep her eyes on the wrecked vehicle through the salt-encrusted windscreen, she groped blindly for the radio microphone. She must call Jerry! He would know what to do.

With a rush of relief she heard the crackle of the radio above the whine of the four-wheel-drive engine.

'Jerry? Jerry? Are you there? This is Alison. Come in, please. Over.'

'Alison? Jerry here. We're on our way to Noosa. Is something wrong?'

Her brother's voice steadied her nerves.

'Yes. There's been a four-wheel-drive accident about halfway along Teewah Beach. I'm just going to investi-

gate, but they may need an air ambulance from
Nambour. I'll keep you posted. Over.'

Ahead of her she saw a creek, its water stained to the
colour of strong dark tea by the tannins from the
surrounding forest, and she braced herself for the jolt
and slosh as the minibus passed through it. A moment
later she was back on smooth, flat sand and the
overturned vehicle was looking larger and larger in
front of her. She drove as close as she dared, switched
off the engine and ran down to the water's edge.

The vehicle was lying on its side, half submerged in
water, with the waves foaming and thundering around
it. Alison's stomach contracted into a cold knot of
dismay as she surveyed the wreckage. The driver's side
of the car was completely submerged. If he had been
knocked unconscious in the crash, he would certainly
be drowned by now. Yet there was always a chance that
he had survived the impact and been able to unfasten
his seat belt and keep his head above water. If so, she
must find some way of getting him out.

Wading into the water, she was almost knocked off
her feet as a large, thundering wave surged around her,
waist-high. It felt unexpectedly cold, and she had to
grab at the vehicle's bonnet to keep her balance. She
tried to look in through the front windscreen, but the
surging waves obscured her vision. Perhaps if she
climbed on the bonnet. . .

Just as she was about to do so she gave a gasp of
shock as the front passenger door opened like a trap
door and a muscular, dark-haired man hauled himself
out. He was completely soaked, and his wet shorts and
shirt clung to his body. Alison felt weak with relief at
the sight of him.

'Thank goodness you're all right!' she shouted above

the roar of the wind and waves. 'Is there anybody else in there?'

'Yes, the driver,' he replied tersely. 'He's unconscious, and I think he may have a broken ankle. All I've been able to do so far is hold his head above water, but we need to get him out of here. If you can climb up and hold the door open for me, I think I can manage the rest.'

It was a difficult business. While Alison sat awkwardly braced on the left-hand side of the car's bonnet and held the door open the stranger manoeuvred his companion out of the car. Somehow, like a climber wedged in a chimney, he made his way up with the unconscious man slumped over his shoulder. Then, climbing like a cat, he hauled the other man as gently as possible onto the undamaged rear half of the vehicle.

'All right, you can let the door go now,' he instructed Alison. 'Then crawl along here carefully and hold him steady while I get down into the water. After that I'll take him on my shoulders in a fireman's lift.'

It was a wet, precarious job, and she was morbidly afraid of knocking the injured man into the surging waves below, but somehow they accomplished it.

'OK. Let's get him up to your bus and see how badly hurt he is. Have you got a radio?'

'Yes,' gasped Alison as she floundered through the waves beside him, trying to keep pace with him. 'I've already called my brother and alerted him that there's been an accident. They'll be standing by.'

'Good work,' said the stranger approvingly.

To Alison's immense relief, the injured man stirred and groaned as they lifted him into the passenger section of the bus. He was bleeding freely from a wound on his head, and the trickle of scarlet mingled with the sea water on his face looked alarming, but his rescuer caught Alison's horrified gaze and gripped her shoulder reassuringly.

'Don't worry, it's only a superficial wound,' he said. 'It'll need a few stitches, but nothing more, and I doubt if he's suffered any serious head injuries. Can you hear us, Quentin?'

Ridiculously long eyelashes fluttered, revealing eyes as vividly blue as Alison's own. The man groaned again.

'You and your bloody films, Rod,' he complained bitterly. 'I ought to get danger money. And what about my ankle? God, it's killing me! Can't you do something?'

'I'll take a look at it,' promised the other man.

Alison was only too happy to leave the responsibility to him. While he was rummaging through her first-aid kit and examining the patient she called Jerry again on the radio.

'Jerry? Alison here. There were two people in the wreck. One seems to be all right. The other one has injuries, but I don't know how bad yet. A cut that needs stitching and a possible fractured ankle. I'll call you as soon as we have more news. Over.'

The air in the back of the bus was turning positively blue with oaths and groans and muffled complaints by the time Jerry confirmed that the rescue helicopter was on its way. Setting down the microphone, Alison turned around and saw to her relief that the man had already bandaged his friend's head and was now busy binding the swollen ankle with a cloth and packing ice from the drink cooler around it.

'I'm so glad you know what to do,' said Alison ruefully. 'I've taken a first-aid course, but I've never had to deal with anything worse than sunburn or insect bites until now. It's just as well you were here. I'm afraid I would have been absolutely useless on my own.'

'Don't worry about it. As it was, you probably saved our lives, arriving when you did. And you didn't panic out there in the sea. I think we made a pretty good team.'

He gave her a brief, abstracted smile, and then turned back to his patient. For some reason that smile disturbed Alison deeply, and she felt herself flushing. Telling herself fiercely not to be an idiot, she climbed out of the cockpit, took a few steps down the aisle and sat down on one of the seats.

'Is there anything else I can get you?' she asked. 'Something cold to drink, perhaps?'

'I think Quentin should only have water, in case he needs surgery on that ankle, but I'd be glad of something in a moment, when I've finished dealing with it. I suspect it's only a matter of severely torn ligaments, but there may be a broken fibula as well.'

As he spoke he was busy bandaging the ankle and then elevating the patient's leg on a couple of folded towels taken from the back seat. Privately Alison thought that the injured man looked ghastly—pale, sweaty and in considerable pain. So how could his companion remain so unruffled? Unless. . .

'Are you a doctor?' blurted out Alison.

He looked amused.

'No, I'm a businessman.'

'Then, where did you learn to do that so well?'

'The first time I dealt with a fractured ankle was in the Swiss Alps on a mountaineering holiday. I've had to do it on several occasions since then. Once in the jungle in Vanuatu, once in the Andes and once in Tibet. Believe me, the conditions in this bus are luxurious compared to those.'

Alison blinked. What kind of business was he in that it would take him to places as diverse as Vanuatu and

Tibet? Places where she had the vague impression that not much trading took place anyway? Or did he simply like to travel in remote areas? A quickening of interest stirred inside her. She had always wanted to travel to exotic places too, but she had married at nineteen. Her lips twisted bitterly. Why waste her time thinking about that when she should be making the injured man more comfortable?

'I'll get you some water,' she said, rising to her feet.

She was glad of something to keep her occupied. As she set out the plastic mugs on the floor and poured chilled water from the Thermos flask she studied the men covertly.

Quentin, the injured one, was by far the more handsome of the two, with his damp, wavy blond hair, vivid blue eyes and chiselled features. Yet there was something plastic and insincere about him that made Alison instinctively dislike him.

Having married an actor herself, she had come to recognise the compulsive need that some men had to charm every female in sight. Even though he was obviously in pain, Quentin made a ridiculous effort to flirt with her. When she handed him the cup his fingers touched hers for a fraction too long, and he gave her a consciously gallant and grateful smile.

'Thank you, sweetheart.'

Alison gritted her teeth and fought down an urge to dash the water in his face. Luckily the other man didn't try any stupid tricks of that kind, although if Alison hadn't been off men—permanently and painfully—she would have said that he was by far the more danger-ously attractive of the two. He was an inch or two over six feet, with a tough, muscular physique and the kind of raw, primitive presence that would make any woman feel a heady rush of excitement.

It was not that he was exactly handsome. Far from it. His features were too rugged, with those cruelly high cheekbones, the grim mouth and the hooded grey eyes that were rimmed by a fine network of lines as if they were used to staring into immense distances. Even his hair, which was currently soaked and clinging to his scalp, showed threads of silver against the blackness. But the overall effect was alarmingly potent. Just looking at him made Alison's heart beat unevenly.

Suddenly, as if conscious of her gaze, he turned and looked at her with a faint, quizzical expression. She felt the blood rush up into her cheeks.

'I'm sorry,' he said. 'I suppose I've been forgetting the usual courtesies. It's time we introduced ourselves. I'm Rod Swift and this is Quentin Gellibrand.'

Swift? Swift? The name rang a distant bell, but she couldn't place him. She lived such a remote life here that even if he was well known she would be the last person to guess it. And Quentin Gellibrand? That meant nothing to her either, although Quentin was looking faintly piqued, as though she should have recognised the name.

'I'm Alison Brent,' she replied, holding out her hand to each of them in turn.

With a faint, ironical smile she realised that if she had mentioned the name she had once been known by, they would probably have recognised her immediately too. Or was she still famous in the outside world? It was all so long ago that perhaps people had forgotten her by now. She hoped so! She had always hated the publicity.

'Hi.'

'Hello, Alison.'

Quentin's handshake was cool, slightly clammy, lingering. It made her feel sick. Rod's was brief, warm and matter-of-fact, but it disturbed her deeply. Oh, why couldn't the helicopter from Nambour arrive, and rescue not only Quentin but her? She wanted to be out of this situation, wanted passionately to be back in her own cabin in the hills behind Teewah Beach, with the door safely shut against men like Rod Swift.

It was nearly an hour before they heard the whir of the motors above them and saw sand flying in a circle of stinging particles. Alison felt a huge sense of relief when the rescue crew confirmed that Quentin didn't seem seriously injured apart from his ankle. She felt even more relieved at the prospect that she was now going to see the last of Rod Swift. Except that, to her incredulous indignation, he refused to leave with the helicopter.

'Do you want us to take you to Nambour Hospital for a check-up too?' asked the pilot, once Quentin was safely aboard.

'No, don't worry, I'm as fit as a flea,' said Rod. 'I'll find my own way back.'

'But—' began Alison indignantly.

'That's good,' said the pilot with relief. 'She'll fly better without the extra weight. Well, see you both later, then.'

Alison made one more desperate try.

'Look, there are no roads where I live!' she cried. 'And the tide's probably come in by now. We won't be able to get along the beach to Noosa, so you'll be stranded until tomorrow.'

'That's fine with me,' said Rod. 'If it's not convenient for you to put me up for the night, I'll just sleep outside.'

Alison was still simmering with annoyance half an hour later as she drove along the sands towards her cabin. An innate sense of decency and hospitality had made it impossible for her to argue any further, but she couldn't pretend to be pleased by the situation.

Obviously Quentin had needed to get to hospital as fast as possible, and she hadn't wanted to make things harder for him by throwing a scene about it. All the same, she felt angry at the way Rod had foisted his company on her.

It wouldn't have been so bad if her brother Jerry and sister-in-law Lyn had been at home. Their cabin was only fifty metres away from hers, and she knew that they would have been only too glad to take Rod in as an overnight guest. But Jerry and Lyn had taken Cathy into Noosa for the weekend, and now Alison was going to be stranded with this wretched stranger overnight and her nearest neighbour was fifteen miles away! For once she felt a brief wave of anger at the results of her self-enforced seclusion.

'Is something bothering you?' asked Rod mildly.

'No!' she snapped.

'I'm perfectly happy to camp out.'

'Oh, don't be so stupid!' she exclaimed in exasperation. 'I'd feel ridiculous making you do that. You can have my brother Jerry's place. He and his wife are away for the weekend.'

'Are you sure they won't mind?'

'I'm sure.'

The rest of the drive passed in silence, although it would have been difficult to talk anyway above the noise of the engine and the roar of the sea.

Only when she turned onto the bumpy track that led up through the sand hills to her cabin did Alison feel a brief twinge of conscience at the way she was behaving. This was no way to run a tour business! No, forget the tour business! It was no way to run your life! Had she really become so suspicious and hostile towards strangers that she couldn't even offer someone shelter after an accident? Suddenly she felt ashamed and uncomfortable.

'Look, I'm sorry if I was rude,' she muttered. 'We don't get many visitors out this way, and I've grown used to my own company. Of course you're welcome to stay.'

He looked at her thoughtfully.

'Thank you,' he said. 'You needn't be afraid of me— I'm not going to harm you in any way.'

'I didn't think you were,' she said, darting him a quick glance and looking away again.

To her dismay, her voice had sounded hoarse and unfamiliar. She found herself blushing again. What's the matter with you? she asked herself savagely. You've taken lots of men on tours to Fraser Island and you've never turned into a gibbering idiot like this! Calm down!

She parked the minibus under the rough aluminium shelter next to her hut and climbed out. Rod followed suit and looked around him with interest at the two cabins set fifty metres apart, each with a wide veranda and a stunning view of the ocean.

'Are there only the three of you who live here?' he asked with interest. 'You and your brother and his wife?'

'No, four. There's my daughter too. She's away at the moment.'

He looked startled, almost disappointed. Or was she imagining it?

'Your husband's away?'

'My husband's dead!' she flared. Then she could have kicked herself for saying it. It would have been better to lie to him, to pretend that Harley was still alive, that he lived here. It would have given her some feeling of protection against the unwilling tingle of attraction she felt towards this man. She saw that he was eyeing her keenly now, as if trying to appraise what her husband's death had meant to her.

'I'm sorry,' he murmured.

'Don't be! It was a long time ago.'

It was a harmless enough statement, but his disconcertingly direct gaze made her feel as if she had said far too much. She clamped her mouth shut so hard that her teeth ached, and turned abruptly away from him .

'I ought to do something about getting dinner ready,' she said jerkily over her shoulder. 'This is my cabin here. The other one belongs to Lyn and Jerry. Why don't you sit on their front porch and I'll bring you a cold drink and some food? I won't be long.'

He strolled lazily after her and caught her by the arm.

'Why don't you let me cook?' he offered. 'It's the least I can do after all the trouble I've caused you.'

She swung round to face him, feeling close to panic. It wasn't only the warm grip of his fingers on her arm, but something about his whole presence that made every nerve in her body quiver.

'No, it's all right. You needn't bother. Anyway, the place is a bit of a mess—Cathy's toys. . . And I've just remembered. I've only got tinned stuff. I don't bother much about meals when she's away. Look, we'll get something from Lyn and Jerry's place, they won't mind, OK?'

She was aware that she was talking in a fast, staccato voice, quite unlike her usual one, but the thought of Rod Swift invading her private space made her feel unreasonably alarmed. This cabin was her sanctuary, her refuge from the world, and she had decided long ago that no man was going to get near her again. No man was going to hurt her. Ever.

If Rod knew how close she was to the edge of panic,

he didn't show it. He simply flashed her a careless smile and jerked his head towards the other cabin.

'That's fine with me. And if we're pinching food from Lyn and Jerry, do you think your brother could lend me some clothes as well? I'm still pretty wet.'

She flushed crimson at this further evidence of how much he had unsettled her.

'Of course. It was silly of me not to think of it sooner. Jerry's about your size, so just take whatever you need.'

'Good.' He smiled at her. 'You're pretty wet too. Why don't you get changed as well and we'll meet on the porch for dinner in an hour's time? My place. My treat.'

Her heart sank. She knew he was only teasing her, but she felt as gauche and uncomfortable as a fifteen-year-old on her first date. Half of her wanted to respond easily and naturally, to tease him back, to make some light-hearted reference to drinking champagne or dancing the night away. Once, millions of years ago, before she had met Harley, she would have done that. Now she could only stare at him in dismay, backing away one step at a time and nodding awkwardly.

'All right,' she said in a strained voice. 'I'll meet you in an hour's time.'

She fled inside her cabin and stood with her back against the door, her heart thumping. What an idiot he must think she was! Had she completely lost the ability to behave naturally with men? It wouldn't be so bad if she didn't have this heightened awareness of his masculinity. . .

'Alison?' His voice was low, throbbing, slightly hoarse. Even muffled by the thickness of the door it had an unmistakable resonance of command. Reluctantly she turned the handle and looked out.

'What is it?' she asked.

'Wear something pretty, won't you?'

Fifty minutes later she had showered and washed her hair and was hovering indecisively in front of the open door of her wardrobe. Her fingers strayed restlessly down over the three shelves that held the scanty collection of clothes that she wore for her work as a tour guide. Yet somehow none of the washed out old T-shirts, shorts or beach trousers appealed to her.

She didn't want Rod to think that he only had to snap his fingers and she would obey his commands like an eager Labrador puppy, but on the other hand she was awfully tired of those faded old salty things! Just for an instant a feeling of excitement stirred inside her as she wondered what it would feel like to be an ordinary woman going out on a date with a very special man.

Her fingers strayed to the hanger that held her one good dress—a gauzy confection of pale cream muslin printed with large blue flowers that she wore when she went to see the bank manager in Noosa. She hesitated.

'Oh, what the hell?' she said aloud, and with uncharacteristic recklessness she pulled it off the hanger.

When she strolled across the fifty metres of sandy ground between the two cabins ten minutes later, she came to a halt and gave a gasp of surprise. Above the distant roaring of the sea the sounds of a string quartet floated, clear and bright and lively. Vivaldi, wasn't it? He must have borrowed Jerry's portable CD player, but how extraordinary to play something so romantic! An incredulous smile parted her lips and she advanced a few steps further.

To her surprise she saw that the plastic table on the porch was draped with a vivid Ken Done cloth in bright blue and orange and hot pink, while the table was laid with Lyn's best china and two fluted champagne glasses.

I wonder why we never eat like that, she thought with something similar to envy. It would be so easy with this amazing scenery all around us, and Lyn would love it, but Jerry and I are always too busy. It's always plastic plates with three or four charred sausages, some tinned potato salad and a can of Coke for us. Perhaps we ought to try harder?

A twinge of nostalgia went through her, for a different way of life. For a brief moment she saw herself as a bird, fluttering wildly in a cage, trying to escape from this trap she had chosen. No, no, that was wrong! She had come here to regain her freedom. . .

Rod emerged from the cabin dressed in a pair of beige shorts and a crisp brown and white checked shirt which Alison had given Jerry for his last birthday. She felt a momentary pang of indignation at the sight of that shirt. Why should Rod help himself to the best garment in Tom's wardrobe? Why couldn't he be satisfied with something ordinary?

She felt even more indignant when she saw that he was carrying a silver ice bucket with a bottle of champagne in it. For a stranger to expect food and shelter after an accident was one thing, but to take luxury items from his absent host's store cupboard was quite another! Her thoughts must have shown in her face, for Rod gave her a brief, flickering smile as he set the ice bucket down on the table.

'If you're worrying about what your brother would say, please don't, he said lazily. 'I have a very good cellar and I promise I'll send him a crate of French champagne to replace this. And some shirts too, if you like.'

Alison stiffened as he moved towards her, but he simply held out a chair for her and pushed it in with practised ease.

'Will you have some champagne?' he asked.

'I suppose so,' she agreed ungraciously.

Deftly he removed the foil, untwisted the wire and eased out the cork. There was a faint pop, a smoky trail of vapour rose into the air and the chill wine bubbled into the glass.

In spite of her hostility, Alison felt a strange stirring of excitement. If things had been different, it might have been very, very pleasant to sit out here on a summer evening, with the sky turning the colour of lavender and wild rose and this strange, vital, disturbing man looking at her through narrowed grey eyes across the table.

'Well, here's to you,' he said, raising his glass. 'May all your dreams come true.'

'I don't have any dreams,' said Alison bleakly, and took a swift gulp of champagne.

His eyebrows rose at that, and she noticed that they were thick and dark and almost threatening.

'None at all?' he demanded. 'What happened? Have they all come true already? Or did you get burnt out and give up on them?'

'What do you think?' Then, recovering herself, she took another slow, reflective sip of the champagne and sighed. 'I'm sorry, I didn't mean to snap. Let's just say that I came to terms with reality.'

'Reality. Well, on the face of it, your version of reality doesn't look too bad. You live in a magnificent location.'

'Yes,' she agreed dully.

'Amazing scenery, an interesting job, surrounded by people you love.'

A spasm crossed her face.

'Oh, so that's it, is it? Someone you love has let you down.'

Alison lost her temper.

'Who the hell do you think you are?' she demanded angrily. 'Just because I helped to get you out of the sea doesn't mean I have to tell you the entire story of my life! What business is it of yours anyway? Why should I talk to you about my deepest feelings?'

'What could be more worth talking about? Look, you and I went through a major experience today. I was that close to dying.' He held up his index and middle finger as if they were glued together. 'And you saved me. It's not the first time that kind of thing has happened to me, and, given the sort of life I lead, it probably won't be the last.

'Well, in my experience, moments like that create a pretty intense bonding between people. If you owe someone your life, you want to cut out all the social garbage and make a close friend of them immediately. That's what I want anyway. To get to know you.'

Get to know me? thought Alison with a suffocating sense of alarm. For an instant she thought of what that would mean. Talking to this man, trusting him, raking up everything that had happened in the past and confiding in him about it. No! No! She couldn't do it— couldn't risk it. And yet she felt a tug of longing so acute that trying to battle it was as hard as trying to fight a dangerous rip that was carrying her out to sea. She took a long, unsteady breath.

'You don't owe me anything,' she said flatly. 'I only did what any decent person would have done.'

He looked disappointed.

'Maybe,' he said with a shrug. 'But I don't understand why you're clamming up like this, why you're so scared of me.'

'I'm not scared of you.'

He tried another tack.

'Don't you get lonely, living here?'

'No.' She hesitated, biting her lip.

Once that would have been the truth. When she had first come here for refuge she had been glad of the remoteness, the distance that separated her from the rest of society. The only other people here had been Jerry and Lyn and one other family, the Campbells, who all knew her true identity. No, she certainly hadn't been lonely then. But lately it had been a different matter, especially since the Campbells had moved.

'No, I don't find it lonely,' she repeated, a shade too emphatically. 'I see plenty of tourists, you know.'

Rod shrugged, clearly unimpressed.

'Tourists come and go. It's hardly a long-term relationship, is it?'

'What of it?' She knew that she was being prickly and almost rude, but she couldn't stop herself. She hated the way he was probing at these deep-rooted insecurities, like a dentist working on a raw nerve. 'Look, shall I help you bring out the food?'

'It's OK,' he said, rising to his feet and walking towards the door with his long, loose-limbed stride. 'It's all organised.'

He returned shortly afterwards with a tray of nibbles. Corn chips, an avocado dip, smoked oysters, olives, seaweed crackers. Alison couldn't help being disarmed by all the trouble he had taken, and she gave him a faint, uncertain smile as she began to eat.

'What about your daughter?' he asked in a conversational tone.

'What about her?'

'What's her name? How old is she? What's she like?'

Alison felt her face light up at the mere thought of her boisterous offspring. Unconsciously her voice dropped back to its usual warm, husky tones.

'Her name is Cathy. She's just turned six. She has reddish hair like mine, blue eyes, a little dusting of freckles across her nose and half her front teeth are missing at the moment. She's as bright as a button, but a little demon—so strong-willed she won't take no for an answer.'

Rod gave a hoarse chuckle.

'Good for her! She'll get what she wants out of life.'

'Yes, I suppose she will,' said Alison with a pensive sigh. What Cathy wanted at the moment was to go to school in Tewantin. Alison had other ideas, and they were locked in one of their fiercest struggles yet over the issue.

'Where does she go to school?' asked Rod, as if he had read her mind.

'She doesn't yet,' retorted Alison with a touch of exasperation. 'I'm planning to start her on the School of the Air program for kids living in isolated places this year. She's well advanced and I'm sure she'll cope. She's already reading and writing.'

'Why don't you just move into Noosa or Tewantin?' he asked. 'You could still run tours from there, couldn't you?'

'I could, but why should I? I don't want to live in a town. I'm happy here. Cathy's happy!'

'But does she have any other kids to play with?' he persisted. 'Cousins, friends?'

'No. Jerry and Lyn couldn't have any children, but Lyn adores Cathy. Sometimes she takes her to Noosa for the weekend, so she does get contact with other children. She's fine, honestly. And so am I.'

Rod raised his eyebrows at the obvious annoyance in her tone.

'I didn't mean to subject you to an inquisition,' he

said drily. 'If you've finished with those things I'll bring out the main course.'

Alison sat in silence as he vanished inside the cabin. She felt too upset and confused to offer him any help, and could only wish passionately that he had never come here. Why did he have this uncanny knack of uncovering her deepest anxieties? And why did she feel such a heightened awareness of his masculinity, the force of his will, the potent, inescapable aura of confidence that emanated from him?

Suddenly she had the despairing conviction that if he really wanted to know all about her, he would never give up. It simply wasn't in his nature. He would keep on questioning her, chipping away at her, until he had extracted every fragment of information about her. A momentary warmth sparked through her—after all, it was rather flattering to think that he was interested— then her face shadowed.

Plenty of men had been interested in the past. Most of them had wanted one of two things. To go to bed with her for a single night or to get the exclusive story about Harley Winchester's death from her. Her mouth puckered as if she had sucked on a sour lemon. If Rod Swift was after either of those things, he had better just watch out!

Yet it seemed that Rod wasn't after anything. He was whistling carelessly under his breath as he returned with two dinner plates, each containing a foil parcel, and set them down on the table. Moments later he returned with bowls of noodles and salad. Then he poured more champagne into both their glasses.

'*Bon appetit!*' he said, deftly unwrapping his foil parcel with his fork.

'*Bon appetit,*' murmured Alison, following suit.

A delicious aroma of fish and coconut and spices rose

from the package. Gingerly Alison slid the food out on to the plate and began to eat. The sauce was superb, creamy and subtle, exactly complementing the juicy white flesh of the fish.

'This is great,' she marvelled. 'Where did you learn to cook?'

Rod's face split into a reminiscent grin that made him look much younger. A grin of pure mischief and something else, something tough and vulnerable, that flashed for a moment in his eyes.

'It started in my misspent youth when I was seventeen,' he replied drily. 'I was sleeping out in the backyard of a Sydney restaurant and I was so hungry that I pinched some vegetables from a crate there. The proprietor caught me and put me to work washing rice bowls. Later on he fed me properly. Later still he taught me to cook.'

'How did you come to be there?' asked Alison in a concerned voice. 'Did you come from a really poor family?'

A look of grim amusement flitted across Rod's face.

'No, I came from a very wealthy one, actually, but I had just been expelled from my third boarding-school. My father had warned me never to darken his door if I ever got into trouble again, so I didn't.'

'You poor kid!' said Alison heatedly. Whatever trouble Cathy got into, she could never imagine actually turning her away. 'Why did you get expelled?'

Rod shrugged.

'Truancy, insubordination, general bloody-mindedness,' he replied. 'According to the headmaster I had "absolutely no respect for the values of the school or the staff members". He was perfectly right.'

'But your father actually refused to have you back at home once you'd been expelled?'

'Yes.'

'What about your mother? Wouldn't she help you?'

'My mother was dead.' Rod's clipped tone didn't invite any further questions. 'And I was an only child.'

'So what did you do after that?' asked Alison. 'Did you make it up with your father and go to another school?'

He shook his head. 'No, my father wasn't the forgiving kind. I went into partnership with Tan and eventually bought him out. After that I franchised the whole operation under the name Tan's Thai Roadhouses. It's done quite well.'

Quite well! Alison's eyes widened. That was an understatement. In the days when she had lived in the United States, she had seen Tan's Thai Roadhouses from one side of the continent to the other.

'Do you really own those?'

'Not any more. I sold out when they went multinational. I was twenty-seven by then, and I could afford to retire while I went off to enjoy myself for a few years.'

'Travelling in the Andes and Vanuatu and Tibet?' she asked.

He gave her an odd, sidelong look.

'You remembered that?'

'Yes. What were you doing there?'

'A variety of things,' he said with a shrug. 'Mainly mountaineering and deep sea diving.'

Alison's blue eyes narrowed thoughtfully.

'It sounds dangerous.'

'It was. I think I had a death wish.'

'But you don't any more?'

'No.'

To her dismay she found that she was intrigued by him, that she was doing exactly the same thing which he had done to her and which she had resented so much.

Probing, questioning, exploring. Because the truth was that she didn't just want to have a polite, meaningless conversation with him. She wanted to understand him, to go beneath that urbane mask and discover the nature of the wildness that she sensed inside him. She wanted to know why he had felt so angry or driven that he had risked his life in dangerous pursuits. And why he had changed.

Her heart quickened uncomfortably as she realised that she was seriously interested in this man.

'I'll put another CD on,' she said abruptly, rising to her feet. 'That one's finished. What would you like?'

'What would you like?' he countered. 'What kind of music do you enjoy?'

She was aware of his eyes boring into her as she walked across the porch to where the portable CD player sat on an old cupboard. She felt so flustered that she answered honestly, without stopping to think.

'Jazz. I like jazz.'

'Great. So do I. Listen, James Morrison is playing at the Sheraton in Noosa next Saturday. Why don't you come to the concert with me?'

CHAPTER TWO

ALISON looked at him with as much horror as if he had just asked her to strip naked and sit on his lap.

'I couldn't possibly!' she exclaimed.

'Why not? Your husband died a long time ago. I can't see any reason why you shouldn't go to a harmless concert with me—unless there's someone else who might object.'

'There's no one else,' she flared. 'And even if there were I'd make my own choices about what I did and what friends I made.'

He gave her a faint, mocking smile.

'Good. Then there's nothing to stop you coming, is there?'

Alison's mouth opened and closed soundlessly. She felt trapped by this net of words that he was weaving round her.

'I don't want to come!' she blurted out.

Yet even as she spoke she knew that she was lying. An image flashed before her of herself at the Sheraton Rendezvous lounge wearing a new dress, sipping a drink, listening to the blues and perhaps even dancing with Rod's arms around her. He would be a good dancer, she felt sure of that. He was too lithe, too graceful to be anything else. A treacherous ripple of excitement went through her at the thought of swaying in his embrace with soft, sultry music purring in the background.

'Don't you?' he asked mildly.

She darted him a quick, stricken look and felt her

cheeks burn. Could he really tell just by looking at her how strongly she was attracted to him? She suspected that he could.

'No, I don't!'

'Well, how about dinner, then?' he suggested. 'I know a nice little place on Hastings Street where they do great king prawns.'

'No, thank you,' she said frigidly. 'It's kind of you, but I'm too busy with the wilderness tours. Early starts and late finishes don't really mix well with a social life.'

He shrugged. 'No, I suppose not. Oh, well. Never mind.'

The ease with which he accepted her refusal made her feel a pang of something close to disappointment. Obviously he hadn't really been interested in her, but had only wanted to while away an evening. Well, it was lucky that she hadn't been silly enough to accept his invitation.

'I'll get the dessert and coffee,' he said, rising to his feet and clearing away the empty plates. 'No, don't get up. I can manage.'

She sat staring unhappily into the gathering darkness as he vanished inside the cabin. It was a beautiful night, as it nearly always was in these parts. The sky was carpeted with stars, a warm breeze set the palm fronds rustling and the sweet, damp fragrance of an unseen frangipani bush wafted on the night air. In the distance the surf thundered on the beach, and from somewhere behind the cabin came the monotonous croaking of frogs.

Alison let out a long sigh and consciously unclenched her fingers from her champagne glass. A strange, wistful yearning swept over her that was half painful, half pleasurable. She knew perfectly well who was responsible for it. Rod Swift!

Why did he have to come here? she asked herself savagely. I was all right. I was coping. I was getting over it all. And now? Now I'm in turmoil again. Oh, I wish he'd go, I wish he'd go!

'There,' he said, setting down a crystal bowl in front of her with a flourish. 'Chocolate ice cream with Kahlua. And the coffee's perking.'

It was only plain old ice cream from the supermarket, but the liqueur topping and crystal bowl made it special.

'Do you always do everything in style?' asked Alison.

'Yes,' said Rod after a moment's consideration. 'I suppose it's because I hate half measures and I've always been greedy for life. Why settle for something inferior when you can have the best?'

Alison watched him with a mixture of resentment and admiration as he spooned up his ice cream. She couldn't help admiring his vitality and gusto, the relentless appetite for life that seemed to drive him. A few hours ago he had come close to death, but now it was as if that incident had never happened. Instead of being shocked or withdrawn, as many people would have been, he was simply getting on with his life.

But what if a disaster had struck him as dreadful as the one that had happened to her? Wouldn't that have shaken him to the core? No, she thought. He would have just picked himself up and gone on. He wouldn't have fallen to pieces like me. Her mouth quirked bitterly.

'Tell me about your tour business,' he invited, looking up at her. 'How did you get started?'

'There's not much to tell,' she said jerkily. 'I was widowed suddenly and my husband didn't leave any money. My brother Jerry was already running this business and he needed another driver. His wife Lyn is a potter, and she didn't want to take on any extra work, so I offered my services. I needed a job and a place to live.'

'And somewhere to lick your wounds?' asked Rod thoughtfully.

'You could put it that way.'

Her voice was clipped and harsh, not encouraging any further comments or questions. Rod's eyebrows rose and he steered the conversation into less dangerous channels.

'So what do you do most of the time? Tours to Fraser Island?'

'Yes,' she agreed. 'And along the coloured sands of Teewah Beach.'

'And the Fraser Island tour, is that only a day trip?'

'Usually. Sometimes if I have a charter group I stay away overnight, or even for several days.'

'Are you heavily booked at the moment?'

'I'm not booked at all. I'm having four days' leave right now.'

'Could I tempt you out of it? I'm planning to make a film on Fraser Island, and I need to go over there to visit some of the locations we'll be using.'

'A film?'

She couldn't keep the tremor of excitement and alarm out of her voice. It was so long since she had had anything to do with the world of films, but the magic of its call was still as strong as ever. Yet if Rod knew the film world well, wasn't there a risk that he might recognise her? Taking a deep, slow breath, she forced herself to relax. After all, it was years since she had acted in her one and only film.

'Yes,' he agreed. 'You sound startled. Why is that?'

'You said you were a businessman.'

'I am. But I have fingers in a lot of pies. Films are only one of them, but a favourite one, I must admit.'

'That makes a change. Most businessmen are only interested in films if they can get a tax shelter, but you really like them, do you?'

'Yes, I do. I watch hundreds of them, and I always go to the Cannes Film Festival each year.'

'Really? I was—'

She broke off. She had been about to say, I was there seven years ago, perhaps we met? How stupid! She didn't want to get involved in discussions about her past, and, anyway, if she had met Rod Swift there was no way she could ever have forgotten it.

'You were—?' he prompted.

'Nothing. Go on. Tell me about the film you're planning to make on Fraser Island.'

'Well, it's a new version of the Eliza Fraser story. You must know how she was shipwrecked in 1836 and lived there with the Aborigines?'

Alison's reserve slipped away in her interest at what he was saying. She nodded eagerly, her eyes alight.

'Of course. I tell tourists about it all the time, and take them round the sites where she lived. And you're making a film of it? How exciting! Have you cast the part of Eliza Fraser yet?'

'Yes, Marielle Mercer is going to play the lead.'

Was it her imagination or was there a slight constraint in the way he said the name? Alison shot him a swift, attentive glance.

'Marielle Mercer? She's really talented. I saw her in that film version of *Mother Courage* two years ago. She was incredibly powerful.'

Rod looked startled.

'You must be a real film buff, then. That one only had limited release in experimental cinemas.'

'I know,' she said. 'I went to Brisbane to see it.'

'Oh, so you do come out of hiding once in a while?' he asked lightly.

The words 'out of hiding' struck her like a whiplash. She flinched and dropped her gaze.

'Now and then,' she muttered.

Aware of Rod's curious stare, she continued to look down, refusing to meet his eyes.

'At any rate,' he continued smoothly, 'I'm backing a remake with Marielle in the lead. Quentin is directing it. Have you heard of him? Possibly not—he's only just beginning to make a name for himself. He's got a lot of talent, although he can be difficult to work with. We were on our way to Fraser Island to check some likely locations today when we had the accident. I'm only thankful that nobody was seriously hurt.'

'You were lucky,' said Alison. 'He was driving far too fast, and those sudden dips in the sand can be very dangerous. That's not the only hazard either. There are rocks on the beach further north, and you need to go very carefully to avoid them. Not to mention getting bogged or suffering vehicle failure. Good preparation and local knowledge are vital just to survive here.'

'I agree. And that's where you come in.'

'Me?' squeaked Alison.

'Yes,' he said, gazing at her piercingly as if it were the most obvious thing in the world. 'I'm stranded here without a vehicle and you're available for hire as a tour guide. What could be a better combination? I want you to take me to Fraser Island tomorrow.'

I must have been crazy to agree to this, thought Alison as she got dressed the following morning. She had passed an almost sleepless night, mainly because she had been so aware of Rod in the other cabin fifty metres away. Even now she felt as churned up as she had when she went for her first soap opera audition at the age of fourteen. This is stupid, she told herself as she pulled on a faded sage-green buttoned top and a pair of beach trousers and began rubbing sunscreen on her arms and legs. It's just another charter tour. Nothing special.

But that wasn't true and she knew it. For a start, how often had a single person chartered an entire minibus for two days by himself? Never. And when that person was Rod Swift, it was a thousand times more disturbing. Two days! Had she been mad to agree? Yet when she had phoned Jerry in Noosa to ask his advice, he had told her she would be mad to refuse.

Rod hadn't even blinked when she'd told him how much the hiring fee was for two days' exclusive use of the minibus, and now she was trapped. What would they talk about alone together all day? Worse still, when they had to make camp together at night, what would they find to say to each other? She flinched at the thought of such intimacy, but something stirred and fluttered deep inside her that was close to excitement.

On impulse she went back into the bathroom, brushed her hair till it crackled, wove it into a French plait and looked at herself critically in the mirror. She had good bones—the cameramen had always said that she had good bones. A small straight nose, a pointed chin, a classic profile. But even at its best her face had been piquant rather than beautiful. Elfin, the critics used to call it. Now she looked at it in disgust.

She was ordinary, totally ordinary except for the rather unusual colouring of her hair. There was no reason at all why a man like Rod Swift should even give her a second glance. Not that I want him to, she added hastily. But perhaps she was letting herself go? Perhaps a bit of make-up would lift her spirits? Some gold eyeshadow and a touch of blusher high on her cheekbones, and a deep, warm, bronze lipstick? Wasn't her theatrical make-up bag still stuffed away somewhere in the cupboard?

For the next fifteen minutes she had enormous fun. At last she stood back, squirted a great jet of duty free Chanel No. 5 from Jerry and Lyn's New Zealand holiday around her throat and batted her eyelashes seductively at her reflection. A small voice in her head whispered, Why are you doing all this for Rod Swift?

'I'm not!' she said aloud. 'I'm doing it for myself.'

The words rang hollow. Suddenly, infuriated by her own silliness, she pulled a horrible face at herself. The one that always sent Cathy shrieking in delighted terror to hide behind the couch. Tongue out, lower eyelids pulled down, eyes rolled up into her head. Well, at least it reminded her how ridiculous all this was. Feeling more in control of the situation, she clapped a wide-brimmed hat on her head and went out to find Rod.

He was sitting on Jerry and Lyn's front porch with an absorbed frown on his face. She noticed that he was wearing another pair of Jerry's shorts, burgundy this time, and a striped burgundy and white polo top. On the table in front of him orange juice and cereal were laid out, and he was talking earnestly into Jerry's radio phone. He's made himself at home, she thought sourly. Catching sight of her, he finished his call and set down the phone.

'That was the insurance company,' he announced. 'I also rang Nambour Hospital to see how Quentin was getting on.'

Alison felt a twinge of guilt. She had forgotten all about Quentin.

'How is he?'

There was an undertone of impatience in Rod's voice as he answered.

'Not bad at all, considering how hard we hit the water. As I suspected, there are no broken bones, but his foot was trapped under one of the pedals and the ligaments were severely torn. He'll be in plaster for six weeks or so, but they'll be able to put a walking heel under it once the plaster has hardened. Of course, he'll need crutches for a while, but not long. They've stitched his scalp wound and there's no sign of concussion, so he should be out of hospital in a few days.'

'That's a relief,' she said, sitting down.

'Yes, it is. It means that with luck we'll be able to start shooting on schedule the week after next. It would have been an absolute disaster to have our director out of action.'

A troubled frown creased Alison's forehead as she watched Rod vanish inside to fetch the coffee. She knew how expensive film production was. Even a day's delay could be disastrous, pushing a film well over budget. All the same, she wondered if there wasn't something rather callous in Rod's manner. Didn't he seem more concerned for the film than for Quentin?

'Don't you like Quentin?' she asked abruptly when he returned.

'I like his work,' he replied.

'That's not what I asked you.'

'Look, I don't have time to play games,' he said tersely, setting the coffee percolator down at her elbow. 'Quentin overestimated his driving skills and damn near killed himself. I have no sympathy for incompetence. Now, do you mind if we have our breakfast and get moving?'

'I'm sorry I spoke,' muttered Alison in an offended voice.

She saw that he had her brother's pocket calculator

and was punching in numbers. He sighed suddenly and looked up.

'No, I'm the one who should be sorry. I didn't mean to snap at you. Having Quentin out of action even briefly is going to cause me a lot of hassles, but it's not your fault.'

He reached out and patted her hand absent-mindedly. Alison stiffened as if she had been stung. There was nothing flirtatious in that warm grip, so how could it affect her so violently? He wasn't even looking at her, merely scowling down at his calculations, and he certainly wasn't taking any notice of her new hairstyle or make-up.

Well, what did you expect? she asked herself savagely. Did you think he was going to say, Oh, Alison, yours is the face of the century! I'll arrange contracts for you with Revlon and Lancôme. And, by the way, you don't know what that fragrance does to me?

'Oh, one more thing, Alison.'

She brightened.

'I've also phoned one of our camera crew and asked him to meet us at Rainbow Beach before we catch the ferry. He's going to bring me a script, a hand-held video camera and a few other things to replace the stuff that was lost in the accident yesterday. I told him you'd have me there by eight o'clock, OK?'

'OK,' she agreed, fighting down a twinge of resentment at the way he obviously saw her as some kind of useful servant, rather than as a woman.

Pulling a face, she reached for the cereal packet. As she champed her way through a bowl of wheatflakes and tinned peaches she decided that she disliked him thoroughly. It was rather a relief, really. It would make the long trip in his company much easier than if she were constantly aware of that powerful physical attraction she had felt the previous evening. She would simply have to treat him with calm politeness, as if he were any other rather difficult customer.

At first she thought it was working. The routine of checking the vehicle and driving it north to the ferry terminal was soothingly familiar.

As always the hypnotic thunder of the surf and the hum of the minibus's engine sent her into a trancelike state, and she found it easy to do her usual tour guide's spiel. She talked about the history of the area, identified the birds and stopped to show him the rusting hulk of the *Cherry Venture*, a ship which had run aground more than twenty years before. And when they went aboard the orange barge which was to take them to Fraser Island, she lent Rod her binoculars and showed him where to look for dolphins and dugongs in the light green water.

Yet as the low sandbanks came into view, topped by scrubby grey-green vegetation, a feeling close to panic swept over her. Two days alone here with this disturbing man! How would she cope? Could she keep him at arm's length?

'Where do you want to go? What do you want to see?' she asked as she drove off the barge onto the silvery gold sand. 'You haven't really explained anything to me.'

Rod shrugged.

'You can take me on your usual route,' he said. 'Just so long as we end up at Lake Boomanjin at some time today. We've decided to use that as the setting for the Aboriginal encampment. Apart from that, I just want to get a general feeling for the island. To try and understand what it must have seemed like to an Englishwoman stranded here in the nineteenth century.'

'It must have seemed terrifying,' said Alison without hesitation. 'Absolutely terrifying. It would have been so different from everything she had ever known. Just think of England, with its green fields and its picture book cottages, and always a town or a little village over the next hill.

'All right, I know it wasn't a perfect society—there were slums and squalor and poverty—but at least there was order, and there were other people like herself. Imagine coming from all that to this!

'This bright, painful sunlight that hurts your eyes, these trees that must have looked so hard and strange and ugly to English eyes. To the sense of being abandoned so far from your own people, the lack of any food that you were used to, not knowing how to set about building a shelter. And then the dangers!

'Poisonous snakes and packs of marauding dingoes and goannas. Stinging insects, sunburn, heatstroke. Even when she encountered the Aborigines, how did she know whether they'd be friendly or hostile? She couldn't speak their language. She must have been an amazingly brave woman just to keep going in a place like this.'

Rod gave her a strange look.

'You sound as if you're right inside her skin, seeing it with her eyes,' he commented.

Alison gave an embarrassed laugh. It was what she had always done when she was working herself into a character—tried to get under that person's skin, see with her eyes, feel her feelings. Only then could she bring power and conviction to a performance. But sometimes it was an ability that ran away with her, as it had done just now. She brought herself back to reality with a self-conscious shrug.

'I suppose I've had plenty of time to think about her,'

she said, 'bringing tour groups here day in and day out for five years.'

'Do you ever get tired of it?' asked Rod.

She thought about that as she turned the vehicle onto the old sand miners' road and drove cautiously round the bends flanked by the endless grey-green forest.

Images of the island flashed before her like a series of coloured slides: the rainforests, whose innermost gullies hid strange, ancient plants and crystal-clear creeks, the sweetwater lakes with their reed beds and swimming turtles and the clean, rippled white sand on the bottom, the dazzling pink sunrises over miles of empty ocean, the bushland with its goannas and wallabies and snakes, its frogs and cicadas and brightly coloured birds.

And then she thought of the feeling of desolation that sometimes gripped her as she wondered if she would be doing this for the rest of her life.

With a sudden pang of insight, she realised that it wasn't Fraser Island that she was tired of—it was herself. She hadn't realised how dissatisfied she was until Rod had come here, bringing with him the glamorous atmosphere of another world. The world of films and social life and conversation. Not to mention his own highly unsettling masculine presence.

Yes, I am tired of it! she thought suddenly. I'm tired of burying myself in the middle of nowhere and behaving as if my life is over. I'd like to break out, do something reckless, laugh, cry, have feelings again. I'd like to go to bed with him.

The thought slipped out before she could censor it, and was accompanied by a vivid image of herself crushed beneath Rod Swift, both of them naked, slick with sweat and gasping with passion. It shocked her to the core and she blushed hotly.

She saw that he was gazing at her strangely, and for

one agonised second she thought he had looked straight
into her mind. Then belatedly she realised that he was
simply waiting for an answer to his question. The hectic
colour in her cheeks ebbed away and she moistened her
dry lips with her tongue.

'No,' she said unhelpfully. 'I don't get tired of it.'

He shrugged and gave up the attempt to draw her
into conversation.

'Well, what are you going to show me?' he asked.

She took him into the rainforest and they walked
through a cathedral of tree trunks where the filtered
green light fell in dappled patterns of sun on the forest
floor and a thick mulch of rotting leaves deadened all
sound. She showed him damp, spongy mosses and
cycads, which had been growing a thousand years
before the birth of Christ and still sat green and tranquil
on the sandy creek beds.

There was a moment's drama when a huge green
kauri pine cone fell from a treetop and almost hit them,
but otherwise there was no sound in the cool, dank air
except for the whine of mosquitoes, the murmur of
running water and the whisper of a breeze rustling the
leaves overhead.

Rod was silent and watchful, totally absorbed by his
surroundings, so that Alison was surprised when he
took her hand to help her cross a springy moss-covered
log bridge which spanned a gurgling creek. She was
even more surprised when they reached the other side
and he did not let go, even though the track widened
out and became much easier to follow. She stole a
sidelong glance at him, feeling completely disconcerted.

Was he simply trying to save her from a fall? Or did
he have some other motive? His preoccupied look gave
her no clue to his intentions, so that she felt like a
teenager on a first date—keyed up, restless, with a

breathless, fluttering feeling in her midriff and the agonised suspicion that she might be making a total fool of herself. It was almost a relief when they arrived back at the car park and climbed into the minibus.

Fortunately once they reached Lake Boomanjin Rod became completely brisk and practical again. Obviously whenever he was thinking about work there was no room for anything else in his mind.

She could sense his growing impatience as they unpacked the vehicle and put up the two tents. Although he did more than his fair share of the work, he kept looking at his watch. When at last they had finished setting up their camp, he unpacked the bag which the cameraman had given him at Rainbow Beach and carefully checked its contents—video camera, script, notebook, measuring tape and plastic markers.

'You know, you might be able to help me,' he said thoughtfully. 'This is really Quentin's job, but I've got a pretty fair idea of what he was planning to do today.

'We've got some black actors from the Northern Territory arriving next week to play the parts of the Aboriginal tribe. They'll be building traditional bark shelters just before we film the scene, but until the wurlies are erected, there's nothing there except empty sand.

'What I want to do today is set out the markers to show where the Aboriginal bark huts will be and the spot where Eliza Fraser is brought along the shore as a captive. If you could just be Eliza for me, that would help me to judge the distances and the time at least roughly.'

Alison stared at him in dismay. An old, half-forgotten thrill rose inside her at the thought of acting again, even for an audience of one, but it was followed immediately by an unreasoning wave of panic. What if he recognised her?

'I can't!' she blurted out.

He looked at her with a puzzled frown.

'Why not?'

'I. . .well, I can't act,' she babbled. 'I'm just wooden. . .I freeze up. I'd be no good.'

'It doesn't matter, he said impatiently. 'All you have to do is walk through the part and read the lines. I won't even really be looking at you. Why on earth are you making such a fuss about something so simple?'

'Oh, all right,' muttered Alison.

With Rod's piercing grey eyes boring into her, she was beginning to feel that there was more risk of betraying her secret by continuing to argue than by agreeing. Anyway, she told herself comfortingly, it's hardly likely that he'd recognise me, even if he did see my film. I was wearing a dark wig and it was a long time ago. Besides, if I act really atrociously, he'll never guess that I was once a professional. The thought amused her, and she grinned slyly to herself as they set off around the lake's edge.

The sun was blazing down out of a cloudless blue sky as they made their way to the far shore. By the time they reached it they were both dripping with sweat, and even Rod was happy to wade in the shallows and splash a billy full of the brown tannin-stained waters over his head and shoulders. But the moment they finished their ham rolls and fruit he was eager to start work.

'All right, here's the script,' he announced, picking it up and shaking the sand off the pages. 'I just want to get a rough estimate of how much time this scene is going to take and what the film footage is likely to be. I'll put these markers in the sand here, to show where the Aboriginal wurlies will be.

'Now, in the film Eliza and her husband have been captured at spear-point and they're being brought back to the settlement. I just want you to do a walk-through of the scene with me to get some idea of the distance Marielle will have to cover along the beach. You read Eliza's part and I'll read her husband's. If you can act it, so much the better. That will allow for the natural pauses and silences. Have a look over the script and then we'll start.'

Alison took the script, scanned through it and, at Rod's command, began to read. Deliberately she spoke in a flat monotone, rather like the sound of Cathy working laboriously through *Skip the Rabbit*, with frequent stumbles over words and a total disregard for commas, full stops or emotional emphasis. After half a page, Rod stopped her with an irritable exclamation.

'For heaven's sake! You weren't joking about being hopeless, were you? Look, it doesn't matter if you can't put much expression into it, but I do need you at least to get the timing right. Otherwise it's a total waste of effort.'

Alison allowed a hurt expression to spread over her face. 'Breathe sadness,' she remembered her drama teacher saying, 'and you will show sadness.' She caught her breath and let her lower lip quiver.

'I can't help it,' she said huskily. 'Some people just aren't good at acting.'

She turned her head away and blinked, as if to hide a rush of tears. In fact, she was struggling with an overpowering urge to burst out laughing. Suddenly Rod caught her arm.

'I'm sorry,' he said. 'I didn't mean to hurt your feelings. If you really can't do it, we might just as well pack up and go back to the camp.'

Alison should have been pleased, but perversely she

felt a twinge of guilt. Was there really any need for her to spoil Rod's entire afternoon just because of her paranoia? After all, it wasn't really likely that he would recognise her, was it?

'It might just be because I'm nervous and it's my first try,' she said. 'We could do it one more time, if you like.'

'All right,' agreed Rod dubiously.

His obvious lack of enthusiasm nettled her, and she suddenly felt a rash urge to show him just what she could do when she tried. Walking back to their starting point on the beach, she let herself focus totally on the character of Eliza and felt the curious thrill of excitement that always sharpened her senses whenever she was acting.

On the blank sand ahead of her she tried to visualise the bark shelters and the strange, dark, naked figures that were running forward to gape in amazement at her white skin and sodden clothing, then she turned to the man beside her and saw not Rod Swift, but her husband. In ill health, considerably older than herself, suffering from the privations of shipwreck and weeks adrift in an open boat, stumbling as their captors' spears nudged closer.

Her voice came out in a croak of exhaustion, but with an undertone of defiance and bravado and hope.

'Not far now, James. They can't be planning to kill us, or they'd surely have done it sooner. Look, don't the little children look sweet? Oh, I'm sure they're going to feed us, my love, and bind up that coral cut on your leg. Perhaps they'll even help us to get back to civilisation.'

The scene went on, and she found herself imagining every detail of the situation. It was only when they reached the red plastic markers that showed the entrance to the wurlies and she sank down in exhaustion and terror on the sand that she realised Rod was staring at her as if she had two heads.

'What's the matter?' she asked, in her own, normal voice.

He shook his head.

'I can't believe the difference from that first attempt! If you could get over your stage fright, you'd be incredibly talented. Have you ever acted before?'

She almost froze on the spot, instantly regretting her impulsive action.

'No,' she lied.

'Well, you should. Look, I'd like you to consider doing an audition for this film. The part of Eliza Fraser is already cast, but there's a wonderful cameo role which is still not filled, for the daughter of the family who take her in when she's rescued. If you—'

'No!' She sprang to her feet, but her legs were trembling so violently that they would hardly hold her. 'No, I can't. I swore I'd never. . . Don't ask me! Please. Don't ask me.'

Staring at him as if he were about to attack her, she picked up her bag, backed away from him and then turned and ran. Ignoring his shout of protest, she ran halfway round the lakeshore, until her breath was coming in long gulps and the sweat was running off her in rivulets. Only when she reached the track leading up to the campsite did she slow down. Even then she was so agitated that she was almost tempted to climb into the minibus and drive away.

But she couldn't do that. There were no other vehicles here and she couldn't leave Rod stranded. With a surge of exasperation she realised she was trapped, and she clenched her fist and punched the dusty side of the minibus so hard that her hand ached and tears sprang to her eyes.

Why had she yielded to the temptation to show off her talent to Rod? Even worse, why had she run off so impetuously? Now he was bound to question her, and there was no way she could bear to reveal the murky events of the past. Yet when Rod did stroll into the campsite a few minutes later, he spoke in a low, matter-of-fact voice, without the slightest hint of interrogation or reproach.

'I'm sorry I upset you.'

'That's all right,' she said unsteadily. 'I shouldn't have reacted like that. I apologise.'

His hand touched the back of her neck in a reassuring caress, and she felt the tiny hairs leap into life. Every nerve in her body cried out with the longing to relax and surrender to that warm, soothing touch. Instead she stiffened and swung round.

'I don't want to explain,' she said in a rush. 'There's no way I can talk about it, so can we just drop it?'

His face was inscrutable.

'Of course,' he agreed easily. 'Do you think we should start fixing dinner now? How about barbecued steaks and corn on the cob?'

She managed a strained smile.

'That sounds good to me.'

'Great. I'll make a campfire. I know we don't need one, because it's not cold and you've got that little gas stove, but there's always something satisfying about a campfire, isn't there?'

She nodded, grateful for the normality of his manner. A campfire would be pleasant, especially since the sun was beginning to sink low in the sky and the fierce heat of the afternoon was already abating.

Luckily Rod seemed to know what he was doing, so she was able to sit in a folding chair, sipping a cold drink and recovering her poise as he laid the kindling in the stone fireplace. At last, when the orange flames began to leap and crackle, he brought out the folding table and a second chair.

'Let's have the corn as a first course,' he said. 'Then when the fire's burnt down a bit we can barbecue the steaks over the coals.'

'All right.'

'Why don't you set the table and I'll go down to the lake for some water?'

Although he had been so calm about the incident, she felt herself relax even further when he vanished down the track. She began to move about the campsite, performing the soothing, mindless tasks of setting the table with cutlery, glasses, bread and drinks from the ice chest.

With a critical frown she lifted out the plastic bag full of steaks and decided that they were too chilled to bring out their full flavour. They ought to be left out to warm a bit before cooking. Setting them on the table on an enamel plate, with a plastic cover over them to keep off the flies, she walked across to the spot where she had hung their towels and bathing suits to dry when they'd first arrived. She was just unpegging Rod's towel when something caught her gaze out of the corner of her eye. She swung round and let out a shout of alarm.

'No!'

She began to run, yelling at the top of her voice. A tan-coloured shadow loped away between the trees in the gathering dusk. And another. And another. Alison felt her heart thud violently with alarm and indignation as she reached the overturned table and found the steak plate on the ground, empty except for a smear of blood.

She fell instinctively to her knees and began picking up the scattered items, then looked up and felt a lurch of panic as she realised what was happening. The members of the dingo pack had stopped and were beginning to circle and come back, their gold eyes fixed unwinkingly on her.

'Rod!' she called in terror.

'Alison? What is it?'

There was a sound of snapping twigs and muffled running footsteps. He came hurtling over the rise at the top of track, paused to assess the situation, then snatched a burning brand from the fire and ran at the leader of the wild dogs.

'Clear off! Go on, get out of here!'

They scattered, melting into the bush at a sinister, soundless trot. Alison scrambled to her feet, pressed her hand to her chest and gave a shaky laugh.

'I'm sorry, I didn't mean to sound so pathetic, but dingoes give me the creeps. They're not like ordinary dogs, they're really vicious—even though they look so harmless.'

'I know,' agreed Rod, tossing the burning stick back into the fireplace. 'They could easily kill a baby, and a pack of them could probably take out a child or even a small adult. They didn't hurt you, did they?'

To her astonishment, he took her in his arms and hugged her hard, running his hands over her body as if to assure himself that she was uninjured. She shook her head, but her breathing was still rapid and shallow, as much from his nearness as from the fright she had just had.

'No,' she muttered.

She looked up at him, but that was a mistake. In the orange glow of the firelight, with his eyes narrowed in anger and concern and his chest heaving, Rod was dangerously attractive. Especially with his powerful arms around her and his body so close that she could smell the mingled odours of woodsmoke and cologne

and masculine sweat that came off him in waves. A
shudder went through her and she swallowed hard,
trying to drag her eyes away from him.

Too late. He had already seen the attraction she
wanted so desperately to hide and now his own
expression changed. He no longer looked concerned.
Instead a flare of unmistakable arousal gleamed in his
eyes and his mouth twisted sensually. Then, before
Alison had time to utter a squeak of protest, he hauled
her against him and kissed her.

His mouth was fresh, warm, urgent as it claimed hers.
And it felt amazingly comforting and right as his
powerful arms tightened around her. A brief whimper
of disbelief escaped her and then she surrendered
utterly, letting her whole body melt into his embrace.

It was as if she had been possessed by a raging thirst
and had suddenly stumbled into a deep pool of sweet,
refreshing water. To resist him was totally beyond her
power. It would have been like choosing to die of thirst
when every instinct clamoured for life and renewal.

Her lips quivered and then parted. She felt the warm,
insistent pressure of his tongue, and excitement leapt
inside her. Her body arched unconsciously, so that her
breasts brushed against him. He uttered a low groan in
response and suddenly cupped her buttocks with his
hands, thrusting her against him. His hard, masculine
arousal butted unmistakably against her. She should
have been shocked, outraged. Instead she felt a dizzy
impulse to tear off her clothes and drag him down to the
forest floor on top of her.

With a shuddering gasp she wound her arms around
his neck and kissed him back, with all the fervour and
longing of a passionate nature held too long in check. It
had never been like this with Harley. Never. Never. Not
even in the good times. Harley had always been selfish

and rushed, impatient to get over the unnecessary preliminaries of mere kissing to the real action.

But Rod didn't seem to think that there was anything mere about kissing. True, he was aggressive, powerful, demanding. Yet he was also unbelievably sensitive and knowing. Alison had never dreamed a man's touch could bring such aching arousal. His strong, expert fingers were moving all over her bottom and back, exploring every inch of her in a maddening rhythm of caresses that made her shudder against him.

He even found the sensitive spot in her spine at the back of her waist, and trickled his fingers up and down it so that she gasped aloud. A frantic, pulsating warmth began to throb through her loins. I don't know if I can bear much more of this, she thought in a dazed fashion. It's so sensual it's almost excruciating!

Her eyes went dark as her lids fluttered shut and she swayed in Rod's hold, quivering at the provocative pleasure of his hands and mouth upon her. His lips left hers and began to trace a fiery line of kisses away from the edge of her mouth, across her cheek and down her throat. The blood thundered in her ears and she caught her breath as he reached her collarbone and the kisses changed to licks. Long, delicately abrasive caresses that left her skin moist and palpitating in the warm night air.

Only when he began to unbutton her top, with the obvious intention of caressing her breasts, did she finally come to her senses. Her eyes flew open, her entire body stiffened and the panic which had been waiting in the dim outskirts of her mind suddenly hit her like a ten-ton truck.

'No!' she cried, grabbing at his hands as if he were threatening to murder her. 'No, you can't! This has all been a terrible mistake. I didn't mean... I swore I'd never... Oh, leave me alone, can't you? Don't you understand? That's why I came here, so I could be left alone for the rest of my life!'

He held her face cupped in his hands and stared intently down at her.

'You're a strange woman,' he murmured. 'Like some creature from the forest, half shy, half wild, and you remind me of somebody. . .somebody I saw a long time ago. Who are you, Alison?'

CHAPTER THREE

ALISON felt her heart give a lurch of panic, as if she had just stepped out of a plane without a parachute. Fortunately she retained just enough presence of mind to give Rod a feeble smile and a puzzled look.

'What do you mean?' she asked unsteadily. 'I'm just me, Alison Brent. A tour guide operator. Nobody in particular.'

As she spoke, she backed away from him, trying to put distance between herself and the aura of danger that clung about this man. After so long struggling to build a new life for herself, the fear of exposure was more than she could bear. Once again she felt the terrified impulse to retreat, to shut off all contact with the world that had hurt her so badly, to run and hide somewhere safe.

But Rod Swift was advancing towards her, running his hand down her cheek, gazing urgently into her eyes. And the wild hammering of her heart, the unsteady rhythm of her breathing told her that she was anything but safe.

'I could have sworn I had seen you somewhere before,' he murmured in a baffled voice. 'There was something about the look in your eyes as I kissed you. . .'

Alison didn't want to be reminded that he had just kissed her. Didn't want to be reminded either that in all probability he had seen her kissing another man on the celluloid screen in a cinema years ago, in 'one of the most hauntingly beautiful films Australia has ever produced'. She moistened her dry lips with her tongue and gave a small, unconvincing laugh.

'Oh, it was probably just one of those chance resemblances. It happens all the time. You see someone who looks vaguely familiar, and really it's just because they have similar eyes or a similar mouth to somebody else that you already know. But I'm sure we've never met before. How could we have done? You're a successful jetsetter and I'm nobody special.'

'That's just where you're wrong,' he growled, cupping her face in his hands. 'With a talent like that, you're very, very special. And I want you to let me help you, Alison. I can arrange screen tests, publicity—'

He got no further.

'No!' she exclaimed violently. 'I don't want publicity. Don't you understand? I'm never, never going to be in the spotlight ag— Well, I just don't want it, that's all! I'm a quiet person, living a quiet life, and that's the way I like it. Now, can we please drop the subject?'

She twisted out of his grip and moved away. As she did so she became aware that her legs were shaking, and wondered whether Rod had noticed it. He gazed at her so intently that she thought he must have done, but to her surprise he did not press her further.

'All right,' he said at last, moving towards the picnic table. 'I can't force you, but I think it's a terrible waste of all you have to offer. Why don't you give the outside world a chance?'

Alison made no answer, but began opening the ice chest in search of more steak. Luckily she always carried plenty of spare food, and the smell of grilled meat soon filled the night air.

As they ate, Rod tried to draw her into conversation, but she replied disjointedly. And when he tried to coax her into talking about her life before her move to

Teewah, she deliberately changed the subject to other matters—dingoes, sand mining, wild horses, anything to head off the danger.

In the end Rod gave up, and simply sat sipping a glass of red wine with a thoughtful, brooding expression on his face. Even then Alison didn't feel safe. She wondered what madness had possessed her to let him kiss her like that and why she still felt this treacherous tingling of excitement deep inside her as she looked at him.

He rose to his feet to adjust the flame on the Colman lantern and his face was thrown into harsh light and shade by its dazzling brightness. Something about his intent, determined features warned her that he would not give up easily on anything he had set his heart on. If he really tried hard to drag her back to the outside world, would she have the strength of will to resist?

As she watched she saw a cloud of insects fluttering around the fatal attraction of the lamp. Inevitably a moth blundered too close, was singed by the heat and dropped lifeless into the dark. Alison winced in sympathy and something close to fear. I'm as bad as those poor insects, she thought with a pang of misgiving. I know Rod Swift is dangerous, but there's something about him that fascinates me. If I don't break free now, will I fall into the fire too?

Rod glanced at her sharply, as if he had just become aware of her gaze. And then he said the words she had been dreading all evening.

'You're wasted here! You've got so much vitality and warmth and talent beneath that reserved exterior. Why don't you come back and give the outside world another chance? Why don't you audition for my film?'

A surge of emotion swirled in Alison's breast. Apprehension, revulsion, but also an unexpected, fluttery yearning. She thrust them down.

'No,' she said flatly.

Rod's black eyebrows drew together in a scowl.

'All right, I'll leave it for now. But I give you fair warning. I won't give up on this.'

She didn't have to wait long for Rod's next attempt to persuade her. It came on the following day. After several hours' more exploration of Fraser Island, they caught the afternoon ferry and headed back along Teewah Beach. At Rod's request she let him drive.

In the beginning she was apprehensive, knowing all too well the hazards of soft sand and sudden changes in the terrain, but before long she realised that he was extremely skilful and was able to sit back and relax. This left her free to reflect on the events of the past two days, but it was a disturbing process.

Stealing a sidelong glance at Rod's preoccupied features, she bit her lip. It was so hard to know what was going on in his mind, and a sense of confusion and turmoil swept over her. She felt as if her control over her own life was being eroded away, like sand attacked by a powerful current. Even though she had been in Rod's arms last night, and he had kissed her so violently, she had no clue as to what that kiss had meant to him.

For her it had been profoundly disturbing. She couldn't deny that she was powerfully attracted to him, but she certainly didn't want to drift into a meaningless affair with him. And even if it developed into something more, which was wildly unlikely, was she ready to handle a serious relationship? Did she even want such a thing? Wouldn't it just throw her calm, ordered life into chaos? And what about Cathy? Wouldn't it upset her if her mother began going out with a man?

And, even supposing she hurdled all those obstacles, what about the future? She had no reason to suppose that Rod intended to stay in Noosa for any longer than the six weeks needed to complete his film. What then? She didn't even know where he usually lived, for goodness' sake! She had been a fool ever to let him kiss her, and an even bigger fool to let him realise that she had any acting talent. All she wanted to do now was escape from the whole wretched situation!

'When we get back to the cabin, you'll have to excuse me if I leave Jerry and Lyn to entertain you,' she said in a strained, rapid voice. 'I meant to use this four-day break to catch up on our book-keeping. There's so much work to do, I'll have to shut myself up for a couple of days just to deal with it.'

Rod made a rude noise.

'I don't believe you,' he retorted.

Alison cast him a shocked, offended glance. She didn't like being called a liar, even if she was one.

'It's the truth!'

'Is it? Somehow I very much doubt it. It doesn't need clairvoyance to see that you'd rather walk through fire than be alone with me. What's wrong, Alison? Why don't you tell me what's upsetting you? It will do you good to share your feelings.'

'To share your feelings'. The words had a poignant ring to them that made her more conscious than ever of the loneliness of her life. She thought of the endless warm, humid evenings when she sat alone on the front porch, watching the moths blunder into the kerosene lamp, with Cathy asleep inside and the whole, dark, lonely expanse of the Pacific Ocean heaving and roaring on the beach in front of her.

A sense of desolation gripped her now as she thought of it. She had always told herself that she liked the isolation of this life, but sitting here now, with Rod Swift's muscular, suntanned thigh so close that she could almost touch it, she knew it wasn't true.

For one wild moment she wondered what it would be like to have Rod sharing her life. They would go for moonlit walks on the beach, make love in the cabin at night, explore the bush together. But no, she wouldn't stay on here if she were involved with Rod! There would be a different backdrop. Rod was restless, cosmopolitan. He would want to go to places like Sydney and Paris and the Swiss Alps.

Alison's heart quickened as she thought of herself in a stunning evening dress, ascending the steps for the opening of the Cannes Film Festival with Rod's arm proudly around her shoulders, knowing that she was admired, cherished, loved by him. Then cold, brutal reality slapped her in the face. Dream on, Alison, she told herself bitterly. He's probably not the marrying kind anyway. And, even if he were, why would he want to marry you?

She was silent for so long that Rod cast her a frowning, sidelong glance.

'Is anything wrong?'

'No.'

'Then I wish you wouldn't look so worried. Speaking of sharing things, it doesn't all have to be heavy drama, you know. It would be nice to share some fun together. Why don't you change your mind and come to the James Morrison jazz concert?'

'No!'

Her tone was so ferocious that Rod gave a groan of frustration and gripped the wheel as if he wanted to rip it off the steering column.

'You're the most exasperating woman I've ever met, but don't think I'm defeated. I'll find a way of persuading you.'

It was late afternoon when they reached the sandy track leading up to her home. Alison was dreading the prospect of being there alone with Rod, so she felt a surge of relief at the sight of Jerry's small Jeep and the three figures on the front veranda of her brother's cabin.

The moment Rod brought the four-wheel-drive vehicle to a halt, Cathy hurtled down to meet them.

'Mummy! Mummy! You've been gone for ages! Look at my new shoes, aren't they pretty? We had chocolate ice cream at Baskin Robbins, and Auntie Lyn let me play five arcade games. Who's this?'

'My name's Rod Swift,' said Rod, crouching down and extending his hand to Cathy with as much reverence as if she were a countess. 'What's yours?'

Cathy patted her smooth red-gold hair, opened her blue eyes wide and grinned coyly, displaying half an acre of bare pink gum and two or three very new teeth.

'Cathy. Cathy Brent.'

'Hmm. You look as if you've had a lot of dealings with the Tooth Fairy recently. Am I right?'

'Yes! How did you know?'

'I have magical powers,' said Rod solemnly. 'I also act as an agent for the Tooth Fairy on the Sunshine Coast. She asked me to give you this for your last missing tooth. You see, there's a special offer this month, a bonus payment for any kid who loses the top left one in the middle.'

As he spoke he drew a five-dollar note out of the wallet in his back pocket and pressed it into Cathy's hand. Her eyes popped.

'Wow! Thanks!' she exclaimed. 'If I write a note for the Tooth Fairy, will you give it to her?'

'Cathy, that will do,' said Alison with a touch of sharpness. 'Jerry and Lyn are waiting to meet Rod.'

And you won't find it so easy to buy my brother's goodwill, thought Alison sourly as Rod straightened up and strode across with his hand outstretched to meet the bearded, chestnut-haired man who was coming down the sandy track towards him. Lyn, who was short and plump and vivacious, with dark hair, hazel eyes and freckles, stood with her head on one side like an attentive sparrow as Alison performed the introductions.

'Lyn, Jerry, I'd like you to meet Rod Swift. Rod, this is my sister-in-law Lyn and my brother Jerry.'

There was a round of hand-shaking.

'I hear you came to grief on the sands,' said Jerry.

'Yes,' agreed Rod with a grimace. 'It's lucky your sister was there. I would have had a rough job getting Quentin out of the vehicle on my own, but Alison was terrific.'

'Yes, she doesn't have enough confidence in herself,' agreed Jerry, smiling warmly down at his sister. 'But I always knew she'd be resourceful in a tight spot, and she's a capable driver too—she knows this area like the back of her hand. You did the right thing hiring her to take you over to Fraser Island.'

'That's something I wanted to talk to you about,' continued Rod. 'I think we'll be needing more vehicle back-up during the next six weeks while we're filming. I thought you and Alison might be able to help me out.'

'Well, why don't we have a beer and a meal together and then we can discuss it?'

While they ate steak and salad and fried potatoes Lyn plied Rod with questions about his background in a way

Alison would have been too shy to contemplate. All the same, she listened avidly and learnt that he was unmarried—heavens, that obstacle hadn't even occurred to her!—that he normally lived in Sydney, that he travelled a lot and owned a holiday home which he rarely used in Noosa.

'Now, what kind of help do you want from Alison and me?' asked Jerry after they'd finally finished their mango ice cream and coffee.

'Well, it's mainly Alison that I want,' admitted Rod. 'I hope to hire her and a four-wheel-drive minibus for the next six weeks for the exclusive use of the film crew. I'd be prepared to pay—'

He named a figure that made Jerry sit up and whistle, but Alison showed no sign at all of whistling. She was staring at Rod with growing suspicion and resentment.

'Why me? Why not Jerry? He knows the area just as well as I do, or even better.'

'Ah, but he doesn't have your acting talent, does he?'

Jerry and Lyn exchanged startled glances as Rod continued smoothly.

'To tell you the truth, I was hoping I could persuade Alison to audition for a part in the film. She did some script reading for me on the island and she was absolutely brilliant.'

'Yes, but Alison doesn't like the limelight,' said Jerry uneasily.

'Well, she may change her mind. But even if she doesn't want to participate in the film itself, I'm impressed by her driving skills. I think she'd be a great asset to our crew.'

'Well, if Alison's agreeable—' began Jerry.

'I wish you'd all stop talking about me as if I'm not even here!' exclaimed Alison angrily. 'Why couldn't you have asked me this when we were alone together, Rod?'

'Because you would have said no,' he replied blandly.

'I'm saying no now!'

'Besides,' he continued, 'it's a family business, isn't it? Well, in that case, surely your brother and sister-in-law have a right to an opinion on the subject too. I wanted to find out whether they could manage without you, and that sort of thing.'

'I think we could,' said Jerry thoughtfully. 'With what you're offering we could afford to hire another bus, and I'm sure our part-time driver Frank would be glad of some extra work. It's a lot of money, Alison. I think we should listen to what Rod has in mind.'

'I don't want to listen!' snapped Alison.

'You send me to my room when I say that,' said Cathy accusingly.

The other adults smothered grins. Alison's eyes flashed.

'Go on, then,' she muttered. 'Tell us about it. Let's get it over.'

'I would want to hire you for six weeks, as I said, and you'd have to be based in Noosa.'

'Noosa? I'd have to spend six weeks in Noosa? That's out of the question—I'd have nowhere to stay.'

'You could stay in our unit,' put in Lyn.

'No! You use it yourselves every weekend. I couldn't possibly do that.'

'I have a holiday home you could stay in,' said Rod in an offhand tone.

'Well, you needn't think I'm staying with you!' she protested suspiciously.

'I'm not asking you to. My place is down on Noosa Sound, but I also own an investment property which I rent out on holiday lets. It's vacant at the moment and you'd be welcome to use it. It's quite comfortable.'

Defeated on that score, Alison fell back on another objection.

'What about Cathy?' she demanded.

Rod shrugged.

'She could stay with you. It's a good place for kids. There's a pool and a garden and a playground.'

'Yes!' shouted Cathy, jumping up and punching the air with both fists. 'Could I go to school, Mummy? Please, oh, please?'

'Now look what you've done!' exclaimed Alison.

Rage flamed through her as she realised that Rod had done exactly what he'd intended.

'What have I done? I've only put a perfectly reasonable proposal on the table for discussion.'

'He's right, Alison—' began Jerry.

'Oh, you've got it all sewn up between you, haven't you?' she cried, jumping to her feet and pushing back her chair with an ugly scraping sound. 'Except that my answer is no! Do you understand? No, no, no!'

'I hate you, Mummy! You're mean,' shouted Cathy. 'I want to go to Noosa.'

Jerry and Lyn exchanged glances.

'Cathy, come and show Rod your sandpit,' suggested Jerry diplomatically. 'While Auntie Lyn has a talk to your mum about this.'

Ten minutes later Lyn sat sprawled in a shabby armchair in Alison's living-room.

'Look, Alison,' she said, 'if you're worried about having to deal with people again, don't be. It's not as though you've been leading a completely solitary existence. You often go into Noosa to pick up tourists, and you do your shopping there once a month. Besides, it's only Jerry who really loves living here in the wilderness.

You're like me—you need more company and stimulus than you can get here at Teewah. If I didn't have the place in Noosa for weekends, I'd go crazy living here. I think it would do you good to have more company. And Cathy would love it.'

'I know,' agreed Alison, pacing restlessly round the room. 'It's not that. Or only partly that. . . It's him!'

She made a despairing gesture towards the outside world.

'Rod Swift? Don't you like him?'

Alison clutched at the air, as if trying to snatch away a cluster of sticky vines that were engulfing her.

'He. . .he disturbs me, Lyn!'

Lyn flashed her a puzzled look.

'In what way? Physically, do you mean? I can understand that. He's so sexy he practically gives off radiation.'

Alison jerked her head in what might have been a nod.

'Did he try any funny stuff?' asked Lyn with interest.

'Not exactly.'

'Well, did he or didn't he? I can't believe that he'd force himself on you!'

'It wasn't force,' blurted out Alison. 'But. . .he kissed me, Lyn!'

Lyn burst out laughing.

'What's so funny?' demanded Alison with a scowl.

'Nothing. It's just the way you sound so shocked about it. After all, this is the twentieth century, you're an attractive young woman and Rod Swift is a red-blooded man. It's not a crime, you know!'

'Isn't it?' demanded Alison with a short laugh. 'Well, it feels like it. I didn't believe that I'd ever do that with any man again—especially someone I hardly know.'

'Did you enjoy it?' asked Lyn softly.

Alison slumped into an armchair and uttered a faint groan.

'Yes,' she admitted.

'Then what's the problem?'

'That's the problem—the fact that I enjoyed it! It wasn't only kissing either. He wanted me to go to a jazz concert with him. It's hard to believe, but he really seems interested in me as a woman.'

'How outrageous!' said Lyn primly. 'He ought to be horsewhipped.'

Alison gave a reluctant snort of laughter.

'Oh, it's easy for you to poke fun, but the whole thing makes me feel horribly unsettled, Lyn. I thought I had my life so neatly organised here. Now I feel all churned up, wanting crazy things—'

'What kind of things?'

'People. Fun. Contact with the rest of the human race. And things more dangerous things than that. Love? Passion? I must be out of my mind.'

'It all sounds very natural and healthy to me,' said Lyn with a shrug. 'I think you ought to accept his offer. Take the job and go to the concert. What have you got to lose?'

'My peace of mind!' snapped Alison. 'My sanity! And what about Cathy? If we move into Noosa and she goes to school for six weeks, it will only unsettle her when she has to stop.'

'Then stay on in Noosa when the job with Rod finishes,' urged Lyn reasonably. 'There's no reason why you shouldn't.'

'I don't want to.'

'I don't believe you.'

Alison gave an exasperated sigh. This was an argument they had had at least fifty times, and she didn't want to be drawn into it again.

'Well, never mind that now. Anyway, that's not even the most important thing. I think it would disturb Cathy to see her mother racketing around with a man.'

Lyn made a rude noise.

'Oh, that's garbage! What harm can it do her if you have a social life? Actually, I think it would do her good. In my opinion you're far too protective of her and you don't let her see enough people. Besides, Rod's obviously good with kids. Look at that stuff about the Tooth Fairy.'

'That doesn't make it any better,' said Alison stormily. 'What if she gets attached to him? The film will only last for six weeks, and heaven knows what he'll do then. Go back to Sydney, probably. That's the whole trouble—I don't know where all of this is leading.'

'Well, the only way to find out is to suck it and see. Nobody's saying you have to jump into bed with him. In fact you'd be a fool to do that without knowing heaps more about him and being absolutely sure that he's the right man for you. But I do think you ought to give him a chance, Alison. Where's the harm?'

Where's the harm? Alison asked herself the same question the following day as they drove towards Noosa after visiting the farmhouse near Eumundi which was being rented as the headquarters for the film making. She stole a glance at Rod's rugged profile and her spirits sank. The harm is that I might be jumping out of the frying pan into the fire, she admitted to herself. I don't know enough about him, I don't really trust him, but I am dangerously attracted to him.

And the worst of it is that other women seem to feel exactly the same way about him. I don't want to be just a groupie, hanging around and breathing wistful sighs like that poor little production assistant, Sarah. She half twisted in her seat to glance back at the white ginger-bread trim of the farmhouse, rapidly vanishing amid the rolling hills and fields of green sugar cane.

'What do you think of Sarah?' she asked with elaborate casualness.

Rod frowned.

'Which one is she? The pale one with the fair hair and the rabbity teeth who looks like a dying swan? Or the dark-haired one who chews bubble gum and sniffs all the time? I can never remember the names of those production assistants.'

Alison smiled ruefully. At least she was certain that Rod knew her name.

'Oh, never mind.'

'Well, what do you think of our arrangements at the farmhouse?' he asked.

'It's very impressive,' she replied. 'I can't believe how good the screening room is, not to mention all those fax machines and modems and computers you have everywhere.'

'I suppose it was quite an exciting new experience for you.'

Alison smiled ruefully to herself. Not exactly new. And 'exciting' wasn't the word for it either. Yet, after the first chill pang of alarm, she had found it surprisingly easy and pleasant to re-enter that world. The smell of the greasepaint and the heat of the camera lights had brought back a wave of nostalgic memories, not all of them painful.

'Yes, it was,' she said, with an unconscious wistfulness in her tone.

'You can still change your mind about auditioning for the part of Charlotte, you know.'

Instantly her hackles rose.

'No! A deal is a deal. You promised me there would

be no acting and no publicity if I took this job. I'll just be a driver, nothing else, or the whole thing is off.'

Rod shrugged, as if the subject bored him.

'Whatever you say. Well, let's go and take a look at the townhouse. After that we'll have lunch together and you can tell me your decision.'

Alison fell in love with the townhouse the moment she saw it. It was a white two-storey building set in a tourist complex, along with about twenty others, amid landscaped tropical gardens at Noosaville near the Noosa River. Raucous rainbow lorikeets swooped and shrieked in the palm trees and a kidney-shaped jade-green swimming pool was visible through a gap between two of the houses.

Rod produced a key and ushered her into the living-room on the ground floor. Alison stood still, entranced by the gleaming white tiles and the luxurious furniture, so different from the shabby contents of her own cabin. She had a jumbled impression of white cane dining chairs, deep, comfortable loungers in vivid, tropical prints, glossy ornamental trees in terracotta tubs and every electrical appliance known to mankind.

'The kitchen's there,' said Rod, gesturing to a high-tech chef's paradise. 'The laundry and the second bathroom are through there, and there are three bed-rooms and the main bathroom upstairs.'

He led the way up the carpeted stairs and opened a door, revealing a bedroom dominated by a vast bed made of white cane with a green and white bedspread. A ceiling fan swished softly overhead and French doors opened out to a balcony surrounded by tropical vegeta-tion. It looked like an advertisement for a honeymoon suite, and Alison suddenly felt oddly breathless just to be standing there with Rod beside her, staring so intently at the bed. It was almost as if they were honeymooners.

If they were, would he turn to her now with a knowing gleam in his eyes and draw her towards him and kiss her? A long, enthralling kiss that would make fire leap in her groin? Her heart hammered at the thought, and her lips parted unconsciously. She looked up and saw Rod gazing at her with a searching expression. Was it her imagination, or was he leaning down towards her?

His eyes were mere grey slits of light and his mouth was twisted, so that the creases in his cheeks were more marked than ever. The heat of his body came off in waves, and it was all she could do not to reach out and run her hands up his tanned, muscular arms.

How easy it would be to slip her fingers into his open-necked shirt and stroke that broad chest! She could almost feel the warmth of his skin, the roughness of the dark hair, the throb of his heartbeat. Her head swam as he leaned closer. Or did he? Swallowing hard, she broke away and fled to the French doors.

'I'd just like to see the balcony,' she babbled. 'Cathy and I could have breakfast out here in the mornings.'

The mention of her daughter's name was like a talisman to keep her safe. Remember that you're a mother, she told herself sternly. You have responsibilities. You can't go round dizzily fantasising about honeymooners and making love and. . .

Alison almost jumped out of her skin as Rod's arm came around her shoulders. Then she realised that he was simply directing her attention to something on the ground.

'You can see the swimming pool from here,' he said, pointing down to where it stood inside a safety fence which was almost obscured by rustling palm trees. 'Can Cathy swim?'

'No, not yet,' replied Alison disjointedly, shrugging out of Rod's grip. 'Even though we live near the beach, the surf's not a safe place to teach her.'

'Well, I'll teach her here if you like,' offered Rod. 'Or at my place, whichever you'd prefer.'

He was doing it again. Plunging her into these dizzy speculations about the future, talking as if they were going to be together at least for quite a while to come. But why should they be? Why should he concern himself with Cathy, unless he was seriously interested in her mother? Or trying to get under my guard, thought Alison sceptically. I'll have to be careful.

'Could we see the other bedrooms?' she asked in a troubled voice.

There were two other bedrooms, both decorated with whimsical wall plaques of sea stars and mermaids and leaping fish. There was plenty of storage space for toys and clothes and books, and the bedspreads with their colourful palm tree motifs were irresistible. Alison's heart sank. Once Cathy got inside this place, she would never want to leave again. This was only supposed to be a six-week temporary job, but what sort of conflicts was she letting herself in for?

'Do you like it?' asked Rod.

'It's lovely,' she agreed in a leaden voice.

'Well, if you've seen enough, we'll have lunch at the Sheraton and you can think it over and give me your answer.'

Lunch at the Sheraton proved even more disturbing. As they entered the peach and teal-blue building Alison felt a pang of pleasure and excitement. It was not just the atmosphere of the place, with its fountains and fine china, its delicious food and impeccable service, it was the man opposite her, who kept sending out signals of some kind that made her whole body tingle with renewed awareness that she was a woman. And a young, healthy, vibrant one, with ageless instincts bubbling up inside her.

He wasn't even actively flirting with her. If she hadn't been so disturbed, Alison would have admired the skill with which he kept the conversation light and impersonal, talking about films and travel and the tourist industry. Yet a silent dialogue seemed to be going on beneath the surface. A dialogue of looks and smiles and tense, unsettling pauses. I can't go ahead with this, Alison thought. It's too dangerous, too scary, too... I can't go through with it!

'Well?' asked Rod at last, sitting back and wiping his mouth with a napkin. 'Are you going to take the job?'

He had very sensual lips. And extremely white teeth, slightly irregular, which only added to their charm. Appalled at the direction of her thoughts, Alison dragged her attention back to what he had just said.

'Are you going to take the job?' he prompted.

Panic surged through her. She must protect herself, must play safe, must close the door against any chance of getting hurt. She opened her mouth to say no. Rod smiled at her.

'Yes,' she said.

CHAPTER FOUR

ON THE day that her daughter started school, Alison half expected tears, panic, second thoughts. Yet, after a long, strangling hug, Cathy vanished into the Grade One classroom without a backward glance. The only tears, panic and second thoughts were Alison's own. As she stood gazing blurrily at the closed door Lyn, who had come along for moral support, gave her a bracing squeeze on the arm.

'Now don't get upset. She's going to enjoy herself and you should too. Why don't you have a day off? Go to the hairdresser's and get some new clothes before you have to start this job.'

Alison made some disjointed reply, but when her sister-in-law continued to gaze bossily at her she finally ran her fingers through her sun-ravaged hair and sighed.

'Why not?' she agreed meekly.

'Good for you. You go off to Hastings Street, and I'll go to your new place and finish your unpacking.'

As a matter of fact, Alison found it surprisingly pleasant to luxuriate in having her hair shampooed, conditioned and trimmed. While she was under the drier she decided to have a manicure as well. Looking critically at her faded clothes in the mirror, she made another decision.

Two hours later she staggered out of the last of a series of boutiques with a huge armful of parcels. The aqua-blue skirt with the appliquéd top in shades of rust and blue had been so flattering that she had decided to wear it. Her old clothes, along with another four new outfits, were stashed away in various paper parcels and plastic carrier bags and, if it hadn't been for Rod Swift's generous advance payment, her credit card account would have been drastically overdrawn.

Glancing sideways at a mirrored panel in a shop window, she smiled guiltily at herself and then did a double-take.

'What are you doing here?' she demanded, spinning around.

The sudden movement made half her parcels cascade to the ground. Alison dropped to her knees, but Rod was too quick for her. She saw the thick dark hair on the crown of his head, the massive width of his shoulders straining against his striped cotton shirt. Then he straightened up and her heart knocked painfully against her ribs as he smiled the devastating smile that transformed his rugged features.

'Looking for you,' he replied, beginning to redistribute her paper parcels methodically among the plastic carrier bags. 'I called in to see how you were settling in your new home and Lyn told me you had come to Hastings Street.'

Alison made a furious mental note to buy a gag for her sister-in-law's next birthday present. After giving way on the issue of the job and the move to Noosa, she had begun to suffer second thoughts about the wisdom of the whole undertaking. Feeling as if her life were spinning wildly out of control, she had told Lyn only this morning that she intended to keep Rod at a distance. And this was all the support she got!

'Yes. Well, I've finished now,' she said discouragingly. 'I'm just about to go home.'

'All the better. I'll give you a ride.'

'There's no need for that!'

'But there won't be another bus for half an hour, and

you've got all these parcels to carry. It's only common sense.'

She ground her teeth, annoyed to realise that his objections were unanswerable.

'All right, then,' she muttered. 'Thanks. Where's your car?'

'I don't have it, but I do have my speedboat tied up at the Sheraton jetty. I'll take you back to my house and pick up the car. Then I can drive you home.'

'That's far too much trouble,' protested Alison, backing away from him. 'I can easily—'

'It's no trouble at all,' insisted Rod, advancing towards her and extracting the remaining parcels from her defensive clutch. 'I've got nothing better to do.'

'How flattering,' she said, with a touch of acidity.

He seemed amused by her sarcasm. His eyebrows peaked and an unmistakable gleam appeared in his grey eyes.

'No offence intended. Let me rephrase that. I couldn't possibly wish for anything better to do.'

In spite of her agitation, Alison enjoyed the exhilarating experience of skimming over the blue water of the sound, with a halo of white spray flying up around them.

The atmosphere could not have been more tranquil. Several people waved to them from sun loungers on back patios, a canoeist hit by their wash pulled a face of mock indignation at them, and a fisherman bobbing at anchor in an aluminium dinghy paused to raise a lazy hand in greeting.

Even the pelicans which were sunning themselves on the end of Rod's jetty exchanged looks of comical resignation, and waddled obligingly away at the sound of the approaching motor. Two of them took to the air, their black and white bodies and huge yellow beaks unexpectedly graceful, as Rod switched off the engine and brought the speedboat alongside the weathered grey planks.

While he was making the boat fast, Alison looked up with interest and a touch of apprehension at the honey-coloured stucco and glass of Rod's holiday home.

The knowledge that this was his territory made her panic flare up anew. In the beginning they had met in her world, on her terms. Even the holiday home which she was now occupying, although owned by Rod, was neutral ground. But this—this was different. Even though he didn't live here all the year round it was his home, and indefinably threatening because of that. If only he had brought his car when he came in search of her, there would have been no need for her to come here. . .

No need for her to come here! Alison's niggling sense of something odd in Rod's behaviour suddenly hardened into outright suspicion. Had he chosen the speedboat deliberately, just so that she would be forced to come back to his house? And, if so, what would be his next move? An invitation to come up and look at his etchings, which would no doubt be hung above a king-size bed?

If that was his little game, he would soon regret it! Alison had no intention of being manipulated into a casual affair. In fact, her only intention was to climb into Rod's car and be driven away from here as fast as possible. She cast him a wary glance, but he simply smiled at her blandly.

As the churning white bubbles began to subside around the boat's hull he sprang ashore with her carrier bags, set them down on the jetty and reached out one strong brown hand to help her ashore.

'Where do you keep your car?' blurted out Alison.

She was aware that she must sound rude, but she felt

far too unsettled to worry about social niceties. Rod's eyebrows rose lazily at the note of panic in her voice.

'It's in the garage on the other side of that stone wall,' he said, pointing through a thicket of red and yellow hibiscus bushes to a honey-coloured wall, almost obscured by a huge, spreading poinciana tree. 'The quickest way is through the house.'

Clutching her handbag and keeping a wary eye on the rest of her possessions which were in Rod's hands, she followed him up through the leafy garden to the back door.

The air was heavy with the mingled scents of sea water and tropical flowers, and she saw that the brick-paved patio was shaded by a vine-covered pergola which offered welcome protection from the glare of the midday sun. An outdoor table and chairs were arranged invitingly, overlooking the garden, and the thought crossed her mind that in different circumstances it would be a very pleasant place to sit down and have a cool drink.

Fortunately Rod seemed to be in just as much of a hurry as she was. He inserted his key into the knob and opened the French door, ushering her into the air-conditioned living-room. Alison began to relax, feeling that perhaps her suspicions were unfounded.

Then, without warning, Rod set down her parcels on the couch and tapped his teeth with his thumbnail, as if he were trying to recall what he intended to do next.

'The car,' Alison prompted. 'You were going to drive me home.'

'Yes, I know, but there's one other thing before I forget. Quentin was supposed to fax me the revised shooting schedules for next week, and you'll need a copy of them. Once you have those you'll have a much better idea of your timetables and when and where

you'll be needed. Just sit down for a minute and I'll
check the fax machine in my study.'

It might be a legitimate errand, or then again it might
not. Feeling in some strange way that she was safer if
she stayed on her feet, Alison set down her handbag
and prowled around the living-room. She always felt
that you could tell a lot about people from their homes,
but this one baffled her.

It was not dull—far from it. In fact, it gave her the
exotic sense of having dropped down in the midst of a
jungle—most of the furniture was made of cane or
bamboo, there were luxuriant tubs of tropical plants
and an impressive collection of Melanesian artefacts—
presumably from Vanuatu.

Carved wooden statues, miniature outrigger canoes
and ceremonial masks seemed to fill every inch of
available wall or shelf space, although there was no lack
of luxury. A carved teak cabinet on one wall contained
expensive television and hi-fi equipment and there was
a fully equipped minibar in the far corner.

Yet somehow, in spite of the money lavished here,
the room was still oddly impersonal. There were no
books lying around, no clutter, no family photographs.
It was totally unlike Alison's cabin, where one entire
wall was covered with snapshots of herself, Cathy, her
brother and sister-in-law, her parents and even old
friends whom she hadn't seen for years. But Rod
seemed to have absolutely nothing to connect him to
anyone else. Except. . .

Alison's sharp eyes suddenly caught the gleam of a
silver photo frame, half concealed by the fronds of a pot
plant on an occasional table. How odd! The silver frame
certainly didn't match the rest of the décor, and nobody
could see it properly anyway, when it was standing

crooked like that. She moved to straighten it and caught her breath.

There was something familiar about the features of the woman in the photograph, with those intense dark eyes, the sardonic mouth and the hair caught back in a severe chignon. There was something familiar too in the impression of slightly taunting aloofness that the photographer had captured on her face.

'Marielle Mercer!' she exclaimed aloud.

A sudden footstep sounded in the doorway leading to the interior of the house. She looked up and saw Rod standing there, in a rigid pose as though he had been trapped in mid-stride. He was frowning and there was an exasperated twist to his mouth. Striding across to her, he plucked the photo from her hands.

'Yes,' he said curtly. 'It's Marielle. She sent it to me as a present, and it seemed rude not to keep it. I just stuck it down here on the table and forgot about it.'

It was a perfectly reasonable explanation, and yet something about his manner was so ill at ease that Alison wondered if he was lying, or at least concealing something from her. But what? If the photo had been sitting among a dozen others she would have thought nothing of it, but alone and in a silver frame it seemed to take on a disturbing significance. Why should he keep Marielle's photo and nobody else's? Were they lovers? Was that what he was trying to hide from Alison? Worse still, was he trying to seduce her just for some meaningless variety in Marielle's absence?

She was shocked by the twinge of pain that pierced her at that thought.

'Is she your girlfriend?' she blurted out.

'No!' he flared. There was something so harsh in his voice that she believed him. With a conscious effort, he relaxed his grip on the framed photo and set it down, but a certain tension still lingered around his eyes and mouth as he looked at her. 'No, I don't have a girlfriend right now.'

Alison felt breathless at the compelling power of his gaze. All kinds of messages seemed to smoulder in his fathomless dark pupils, and she sensed an urgency about his stance, as if he were consciously resisting the need to drag her into his arms. Swallowing nervously, she tried to lighten the mood.

'What's the problem? Are you too old? Or is there nothing on offer?'

His eyes flashed at that, and there was a touch of resentment in his voice as he answered.

'There's plenty on offer,' he growled. 'But nothing that appeals. Until now.'

This time there was no mistaking the raw desire in his expression as he looked at her. Once again Alison felt as if she were standing on a sandy beach, with a powerful, dangerous current surging around her, sucking the ground from beneath her feet.

'D-did the fax come?' she stammered, dropping her eyes and turning away.

He let out an exasperated sigh, as if he were annoyed by this return to the mundane.

'No, but I phoned Quentin and complained. He told me he'll get the information typed up and sent within the next half-hour.'

'I see,' said Alison, groping blindly for her bag. By now she was thoroughly flustered and wanted only to escape. 'In that case, I'd better go. I can easily collect a copy of the schedule when I come to Eumundi tomorrow.'

Once again Rod was too quick for her, just as he had been in Hastings Street. With a swift movement he picked up one of the plastic carrier bags.

'"Suzanne's Swimwear Boutique".' he read aloud. 'Look, I've got a better idea. Seeing that you're all equipped, why don't you stay and have a swim for half an hour or so? Then, when Quentin's fax arrives, you can take it with you. That way you won't have to worry about rushing out to Eumundi early tomorrow and you can have a bit more time with your daughter.'

Alison glared at him in exasperation. It was so neat, so pat, so infuriating! She opened her mouth to refuse, and then paused. She had the ridiculous suspicion that if she did refuse Rod would find some other devious means of outwitting her. And, after all, what harm could a swim do? If he did try anything unwelcome, she could always pick up one of those Melanesian clubs and brain him with it!

'All right,' she muttered.

Rod looked surprised.

'I thought you'd argue.'

'And I thought that if I did, you'd do what Jerry used to do to me when we were kids.'

'What was that?'

'Grab my toys and hold them out of reach so that I had to keep jumping up for them. He used to find it amusing to watch me lose my temper and go berserk.'

Rod's lips twitched.

'I can imagine. I think I'd find it amusing too. Is there any chance that it might work now?'

He held the shopping bag aloft like a starter's pistol, but Alison merely shook her head with an odd smile, half bitter, half triumphant.

'None at all. These days I never get carried away by violent emotions. I'm one hundred per cent controlled.'

There was a long silence in which a lot seemed to be happening. She became aware of the unsteady rhythm of her heartbeat, of the crazy impulse she had to run at

Rod and hammer furiously at him with her fists as she had done to Jerry during her childhood rages.

She also became aware of a desire totally unlike anything she had ever felt towards her brother. At the age of eight she had wanted to *kill* Jerry, while now, twenty years later, she didn't really want to hurt Rod. With a surge of dismay she realised that she only wanted to launch herself at him with flailing fists in order to find herself caught and held against him. She shivered at the thought.

'I hope you don't mean that,' he said in a low, hoarse voice. 'I'd hate to think of you being a hundred per cent controlled.'

What kind of crazy thing she might have done next, she didn't know, but fortunately Rod's mood seemed to undergo an abrupt change. Before she could do anything he shrugged and smiled, as if he had been playing some intense game and grown tired of it.

'Come and I'll show you a spare bedroom where you can change. The swimming pool's at the side of the house, just through this other set of French doors. You can join me when you're ready.'

The swimming pool was large and kidney-shaped, surrounded by terracotta tiles with carved Balinese statues of elephants and warriors. Rod was already in his swimsuit, standing casually on the far side as she emerged from the house, and she could not help admiring his physique. He had an athlete's body, lean and hard, with broad shoulders and taut, defined abdominal muscles.

Realizing that he was returning her gaze with interest, Alison blushed, flung down her borrowed towel on a lounge chair and dived hastily into the deep end. She had only intended to gain concealment from Rod, but she felt a shock of pleasure at the cool impact of the water on her hot, sticky body. Putting her head down, she did a slow, steady breaststroke up and down the pool.

A moment later a wash of turbulence hit her as Rod dived in and swam towards her. His freestyle was smooth, unobtrusive and very, very fast. Reaching the shallow end, he stood up. As he reared out of the water beside her, shaking his wet hair out of his eyes, Alison felt an involuntary thrill at the mere sight of him. His gaze rested appreciatively on her new, one-piece navy bathing suit.

In the boutique Alison had wondered briefly whether its plunging neckline was really suitable for the mother of a six-year-old. Now, seeing the glint in Rod's eyes, she felt disturbingly certain that it wasn't. Well, it was too late now! She slipped below the waterline until only her throat and head were visible.

'Are you feeling energetic or lazy?' he quizzed.

'Lazy,' she replied.

'Would you like me to get you a lilo so you can float around and take it easy?'

'Mmm, please.'

She didn't realise how tense she was until Rod produced an inflated lilo from the storeroom next to the spa, tossed it into the pool and hoisted her aboard.

'I'm going to swim a few laps, but don't worry if you fall asleep,' he said. 'I'll rescue you if you're showing signs of sunburn or drowning. Now, let me just park you under the shade of the palm trees.'

It was very pleasant to lie with her eyes closed, listening to the rustle of the palm fronds overhead, the soft lap-lap of the water against the tiles and the distant, rhythmic splashing of Rod's freestyle. Up and down, up and down he went, as if he were training to swim to the

Whitsunday Islands and back. Alison's thoughts began to drift like skeins of gossamer.

It's nice here, so peaceful, so civilised, so safe. And Rod really is a very good host. Even if he did look twice at my new bathing suit, he's not trying to take advantage of me at all. Perhaps he really does want us to be friends. Hmm. Friends. If things were different, if there weren't so much holding me back, I'd like to be something much more than just friends with him. . .

She was fathoms deep in a shockingly erotic dream when she had the sensation that the ocean floor had suddenly erupted beneath her. The lilo tipped over and she catapulted into the water amid a shower of bubbles. Choking and gasping, she spluttered back to reality and glared at Rod, who was gripping the lilo with a sly smile.

'You swine!' she coughed indignantly. 'What did you do that for?'

'You've been asleep for the last twenty minutes. It's time you woke up. I've finished my laps and I'm bored.'

'Why couldn't you leave me alone?' she mumbled, still half regretting the vanished dream.

'I didn't want to. Besides, you were talking in your sleep.'

Alison's face flamed.

'Was I really?' she demanded in a stricken voice. Then, catching the unholy glint of amusement in his eyes, she launched herself at him with a cry of outrage. 'You lying hound! Take that! And that!'

There was a flurry of water, bubbles went up her nose, and she felt the unbelievable strength of his grip as he fended her off. Then his grip changed. Everything changed. The world faltered into slow motion as Rod's arms tightened around her and his mouth came down on hers. The lilo bobbed away, the sunlight flared orange through her closed eyelids and there was nothing but their bodies,, moulded together in the buoyant lightness of the pool.

The water felt like cool silk lapping against her waist, but she scarcely noticed it, for every cell in her body was reacting to only one thing. Rod's embrace. Caught in his wet, warm, powerful grip, with his tongue coaxing hers and his hands doing the most wonderful, extraordinary things to her naked back, she felt almost intoxicated with excitement. Strained against him, she could feel the strong, accelerating thump of his heart, could taste the warm freshness of his mouth and, with only the flimsy barriers of their swimsuits between them, could feel immediately the effect she was having on him.

The sudden, wild, hardening leap of his manhood against her sent an answering jolt of passionate warmth through her own body and she whimpered involuntarily, pressing herself against him.

'Alison,' he groaned into her hair. 'Alison, Alison, you don't know what you do to me. Come out of the pool. We'll—'

'Rod?'

The voice was female. A rich, imperious contralto. Swearing violently, Rod released Alison and flung himself into the water just as a dark-haired woman dressed in a red silk trouser suit appeared from inside the house.

'Where are you?' she continued.

'Here. In the pool.'

There was the sound of high-heeled sandals tapping on the tiled surrounds of the pool, then the newcomer draped her arm gracefully round the neck of a stone elephant and leaned forward to observe them.

'Well, well, so you are. And who may this be?'

'Marielle, this is Alison Brent. Alison, I'd like you to meet Marielle Mercer.'

Even without the introduction Alison would have recognised the actress immediately. She had seen that luminous pallor, those expressive dark eyes and the sinuous movements in a dozen films, and found they were even more mesmerising in real life.

Now, to her dismay, she had the uncanny feeling that Marielle was playing the part of a gallant wife who found herself betrayed, but was determined to retain her dignity and fight for her man. The actress's gaze tracked from Alison to Rod and back again, and a look of pain flashed briefly in her eyes, to be replaced at once with an artificially bright smile.

'Well, do come out of the water and let me get to know you,' she invited generously.

Feeling a stab of guilt as painful as if she had just been convicted of mass murder, arson, larceny and grievous bodily harm, Alison hauled herself up the steps. It didn't help when she glanced over her shoulder and saw Rod looking both surly and defensive—the absolute picture of a man caught out.

'Now, just dry off, Alison, and I'll fetch us all some drinks from the kitchen,' offered Marielle.

'There's no need,' growled Rod curtly. 'I was just about to drive Alison home.'

Marielle's dark eyes widened.

'Oh, but I insist. I want to know all about your new friend, darling. How you met and what she's doing here.'

Rod's reply was unexpectedly clipped and dismissive.

'We only met a few days ago. I've employed her to do some driving for the film, that's all.'

Alison gave him a long, burning look. The traitor! Five minutes ago he had been kissing her passionately, and now he was only too anxious to disown her. She was so angry that the possibility of hurting Marielle's feelings didn't even enter her head.

'Do you always kiss your employees when you invite them to swim with you?' she cooed, smiling sweetly at Rod.

Rod winced, Marielle looked appalled, but it was Alison who had the last word.

'Well, go on, *darling*,' she urged. 'Tell us both the truth.'

Marielle looked so stunned and resentful that Alison realised too late how insensitive she had just been. Turning to the other woman, she made a belated attempt to smooth things over.

'I'm sorry about this,' she said awkwardly. 'But Rod never mentioned you to me.'

After that she didn't wait around to hear Rod's explanations, for she felt quite certain they would be threadbare and unconvincing. Snatching up her towel, she marched into the house, locked herself in the bedroom allotted to her and began to get dry. Her fingers were shaking so much that she could scarcely hold the towel, and, in any case, she felt as if the red-hot force of her rage ought to be enough to sizzle her dry in no time.

In the distance she heard the sound of upraised voices, a slammed door, the scurry of high-heeled sandals on the front path and the sudden explosive roar of a car engine. Obviously Marielle was gone. Poor thing! Still, it might make her own exit less embarrassing, and the sooner she left, the better.

It was a pity Lyn had done all that unpacking today, for it would all have to be packed up again. Because as soon as Alison got to Noosaville she was going to ring up and resign from this job, and she and Cathy were moving back to the cabin and she was never, ever going to have dealings with a man again!

She almost split her new top by hauling it over her still wet shoulders. With an exclamation of impatience she tore it off, rubbed herself fiercely with the towel and tried again. Dressed at last, she strapped on her watch with furious, jerky movements and crammed her feet into her sandals. She was just about to open the door when there was a loud rapping on it. It could only be Rod.

'Go away!' she shouted.

'Are you going to open this door, or am I going to break it down?'

'It's your house,' she exclaimed disdainfully. 'I don't suppose you have any more scruples about vandalism than you do about lying.'

'Stop lecturing me and open the damned door!'

Alison hesitated. She would have liked to leave him outside all day, but the disadvantage was that she would then have to stay inside all day. She glanced longingly at the window and ground her teeth. She had no intention of adding to the humiliation she had already suffered by struggling through a large, woody hibiscus bush to escape. Sulkily she turned the key and Rod stormed into the room, fully dressed, but looking damp, rumpled and furious.

'Why the hell did you have to mess things up like that?'

Alison choked with speechless indignation. It was several seconds before she could get any coherent words out.

'You... You... I might say the same to you! What did you think you were doing, kissing me and then acting as if you didn't know me? You slimy hypocrite!

And what about poor Marielle? How do you think she feels?'

'Poor Marielle!' jeered Rod. 'I hope she's suffering, that's all I can say!'

'You swine, you utter swine. You take my breath away. Cheating on your girlfriend and then hoping it upsets her! You're totally heartless, aren't you?'

'She's not my girlfriend!'

'Well, she seems to think she is. She certainly acts as if she is. How did she get into the house, then? And why was she so upset at the thought of your kissing me if she's not your girlfriend?'

Rod took in breath in a long, dragging gulp and ran his fingers through his wet hair.

'It's a long story,' he muttered. 'And one that I don't really want to tell you.'

'I'll bet you don't!' snapped Alison. 'In any case, I don't want to hear it. Just get out of my way. I'm catching a bus back to Noosaville and then— Oh, no! Oh, no!'

'What is it?' he asked, sensing the dismay in her voice.

'It's a quarter to three. I'll never get there in time to pick up Cathy from school.'

'I'll drive you.'

'I don't want—' began Alison, and then gave a groan of exasperation as she realised that she really had no choice.

Rod's car proved to be a gleaming red Porsche, which in her present mood only added to Alison's annoyance. I hate rich men who think the normal laws of good manners and consideration don't apply to them! she thought savagely as he reversed the car out of the garage.

He drove, as he swam, with a minimum of fuss but a

smooth, economical style. No doubt he picked up and discarded women in the same efficient way! Alison's lips hardened into a scornful line, and she glared out the window at the lush tropical gardens and lovingly tended houses that were slipping by.

Yet, in spite of her simmering rage, somewhere deep down she kept expecting Rod to say something—to break the silence, to make some attempt at explanation or apology. Instead he simply stared straight ahead with a furrow between his eyebrows and a brooding twist to his mouth. His complete lack of penitence only fed Alison's anger further.

What upset her most was the feeling that the whole wretched episode was so unfinished. She wanted to shout at Rod, to go on quarrelling, to extract some explanation from him, even if it was only the entirely obvious and humiliating one—that he had hoped to seduce her and keep his steady girlfriend Marielle in ignorance about it. That would be incredibly wounding, but at least she would know where she stood.

As it was, she had the unsatisfactory sense of being left hanging. Well, her pride wouldn't let her reopen the whole, painful issue now. It was better just to keep her mouth shut until they reached Cathy's school and then tell Rod that she was leaving his employment. But it was a pity really. Cathy would be so disappointed, and Alison had even begun to feel that she might enjoy living in Noosa herself.

She clutched her parcels more tightly against her and then looked down at them with a wry grimace. She wouldn't need those any more, not if she was going back to faded old beach clothes and a hermit's life! A surge of desolation swept through her at the thought and she heaved a deep sigh.

'Oh, for heaven's sake!' snarled Rod. Abruptly he

turned the car off the road and brought it to a halt in the parkland that ran along the edge of the river. 'There's nothing to make such a fuss about! This whole incident is ridiculously trivial.'

'It may be ridiculously trivial to you, but it's important to me!' blazed Alison. 'Anyway, I don't have time to sit here talking about it. I have to pick my daughter up from school. Unlike you, I have commitments that mean something to me!'

His eyes leapt with resentment.

'Are you implying that I'm incapable of commitment?'

'Well, that's obvious, isn't it?' she taunted.

'No, it's not! You think you understand what's going on, but you're wrong.'

'Well, whose fault is that?' she flashed back. 'You haven't been exactly forthcoming with explanations, and anyway I don't want to hear them. It's my daughter I'm concerned about, not you.'

Rod glanced at his watch.

'I'll get you there on time—it's not far. Trust me!' Suddenly he turned in his seat and gripped her shoulder. Some of the antagonism went out of his voice and was replaced by a bitter yearning. 'I wish you'd trust me about the whole thing, Alison. I could explain, but it's so complicated, you'd... Well, let me just say this. I swear that Marielle is not my girlfriend. She's not living with me and I'm not in love with her.'

'How did she get into the house if she's not living with you?'

'She must have just walked in off the street. There's nothing extraordinary about it—anyone could have done it. I never keep the front door locked when I'm at home, because I'd only end up locking myself out if I did. The most likely explanation is that she rang the front doorbell and we didn't hear her, so she simply let herself in. My friends do it all the time.'

Alison hunched her shoulders impatiently, feeling obscurely annoyed to hear Marielle described even as a friend.

'Look, it doesn't matter to me anyway,' she burst out untruthfully. 'You could talk all day and it wouldn't make me feel any better about what happened. Now, would you please drive me over to the school to pick up my daughter?'

With an exclamation of impatience, Rod rammed the car into gear and reversed out onto the road with less than his usual dexterity. They passed the rest of the short journey in smouldering silence. It was only when they pulled up outside the school grounds at Tewantin that he spoke again. Fortunately they had arrived in time, and there was no sign yet of any school children emerging from the building.

'Why don't you have dinner with me tomorrow night and we can discuss this whole business like a pair of rational adults?' he urged.

Alison shook her head.

'I'm sorry,' she said bleakly. 'But I don't think there's any point discussing it. And I don't think there's any point in seeing each other again either. Look, I've made a mistake in accepting this job with you, Rod, and I don't want to continue. I'm sorry if that inconveniences you from a practical point of view, but if you really need someone I'm sure my brother Jerry could fill in for me. I can either pay you back the advance you've given me, or hand it over to him—whichever you prefer. But I'm taking Cathy and moving back to the cabin. We'll be leaving tomorrow.'

Her voice broke on the last word and she had to

swallow hard to suppress the painful lump in her throat. To her surprise Rod seized her hands in his.

'You can't,' he growled. 'I won't let you go.'

Half dismayed, half moved, she tried to pull back. His voice was harsh and his eyes blazed as he spoke again.

'Look, I know you think I've deceived you and humiliated you, but that wasn't my intention at all. And it isn't the truth. All I'm asking you to do is to wait, give me a chance to let me prove that I'm not the kind of bastard you obviously think I am. It's only fair to give me a full trial before you convict me.'

Alison was still staring at him in tormented indecision when the clang of the school bell shattered the silence. Hastily she unlocked the car door and climbed out.

'I must go and get Cathy. I'll come back and get my parcels in a moment. Thank you for the ride.'

To her dismay she found that he was beside her, matching her stride for stride. Before she had time to protest, the door of the classroom burst open and a swarm of excited youngsters poured on to the playground.

Foremost among them was Cathy, her neat ginger pigtails now wildly disordered, a smudge of red paint on her cheek, her socks around her ankles, her schoolbag and hat dangling from one hand and her face alight with satisfaction. At the sight of her mother, she let out a whoop of joy and broke into a run.

'Hello, Mummy!' she shouted, flinging herself on Alison. 'Guess what? There are two fish in our classroom and their names are Goldy and Locks and I've been invited to a birthday party on Saturday. It's for my best friend Hannah, she's going to be six like me, except I'm older than she is and she hasn't lost any teeth yet, and I've written a story. Hello, Rod!'

'Hello, Cathy,' said Rod, squatting down beside her and smiling. 'Your mother was in such a rush today that she didn't have time to go home and get her minibus, so I'm giving you a ride home in my car. Is that all right?'

Cathy let out an earsplitting shriek of delight.

'Great!'

If Alison's own feelings towards Rod hadn't been in such turmoil, she might have been touched by the way he set Cathy's sunhat straight on her tumbled hair and carried her bag for her. As it was, she felt a twinge of something close to alarm or jealousy when Cathy positioned herself between them, offered them one grimy paw each and beamed trustingly at them.

This was a mistake, thought Alison anxiously, as she let her daughter tow her across the playground and out of the gate. She'll get attached to him, and then where will I be?

Cathy's eyes opened wide and she gave a sigh of pure bliss when Rod stopped by the red Porsche and unlocked the passenger door for her. After a couple of energetic bounces on the leather seat, she suddenly scrabbled in her schoolbag and produced a large white sheet of paper covered in straggly printing. Leaning forward, she handed it to Alison, but glanced eagerly at both of them.

'Would you like to read my story?' she demanded.

'Cathy, perhaps later—' began Alison.

'No, now!' pleaded Cathy, with the beginning of a whine in her voice. 'Now, now, please, Mummy. Because it's about you and Rod. I want him to hear it too.'

With a sinking feeling of misgiving in the pit of her stomach, Alison looked down at the page.

'Cathy's story

I realy wantd to go to school but I dident think I code an till Rod told Mummy to let me go Rod is Mummys new frend we liv at his howse now the end.'

Alison groaned audibly, and there was a muffled snort of laughter from Rod, hastily changed to a cough. She flashed him a warning glare.

'What's the teacher going to think of that?' she demanded under her breath .

Cathy looked hurt and bewildered.

'Didn't you like my story, Mummy? I worked very hard on it.'

Alison twisted further in her seat, opened her mouth and then stopped. The prospect of explaining the social implications to a six-year-old was far too daunting— especially with Rod sitting beside her, wearing a smirk of unholy amusement on his face. She gave her daughter a wan smile.

'It was a lovely story, darling,' she said in a failing voice. 'Now, put your seat belt on and let's go home.'

Still looking faintly aggrieved, Cathy obeyed. Then another thought struck her.

'I can go to Hannah's birthday party on Saturday, can't I?' she demanded imperiously.

Rod started up the engine and cast Alison a sly, challenging glance before he pulled away from the kerb.

'I'm not sure that that will be possible, Cathy,' he said regretfully. 'Your mother has decided she doesn't like living in Noosa much after all. She's thinking of moving straight back to Teewah Beach.'

There was a moment's outraged silence, then Cathy exploded.

'That's not fair, Mummy!' she wailed. 'You can't do

that! You promised we'd live here at least until the filming ended. It isn't fair! It isn't fair!'

Alison gritted her teeth. What was that poison the South American Indians used? Curare? If she had had an arrow tipped in curare at this moment, she would have shot it joyfully straight into Rod Swift's heart! As it was, she could only glower at him. The calculating swine—to use a six-year-old to do his dirty work for him! Knowing Cathy's expertise in the gentle art of pestering, Alison was quite certain she would be subjected to a relentless barrage of sulks, wheedling and protest.

'Mummy, it isn't fair!' repeated Cathy again.

'Look—' began Alison.

And then she stopped. As she spoke a twinge of guilt went through her. Cathy was right—it wasn't fair. Not fair to her daughter, or her brother, or her sister-in-law, or even to her own standards of integrity. In the past she had always prided herself on being reliable, on keeping to her commitments. And, however unwilling she might be to have any further dealings with Rod Swift, something deep inside her disapproved of the idea of running away. At that moment she knew she was defeated.

'All right, don't get upset,' she said wearily. 'We're not leaving, Cathy, we're staying right here.'

'I had a feeling you might say that,' murmured Rod in a satisfied voice.

His look of triumph annoyed Alison so much that she had to have the last word.

'Of course, I'll be far too busy coping with Cathy's social life from now on to have time for one of my own. From here on, our dealings will have to be strictly business, Mr Swift.'

His eyebrows rose at that, and there was something

FREE!

FOUR FREE
specially selected
Mills & Boon Romances
PLUS a ladies wallet,
when you return this card...

There's no catch

You're under no obligation to buy anything. We charge you nothing for your first shipment. And you don't have to make any minimum number of purchases - not even one!

The fact is thousands of readers enjoy receiving books by mail from the Reader Service. They like the convenience of home delivery and they like getting the best new novels at least a month before they're available in the shops. And, of course, postage and packing is completely FREE!

We hope that after receiving your free books and gift you'll want to remain a subscriber. But the choice is yours - to continue or cancel, anytime at all! So why not take us up on our invitation, with no risk of any kind. You'll be glad you did!

See over for details...

YES!

Please send me four FREE Mills & Boon Romances and my FREE ladies wallet. I understand that unless you hear from me, I will receive six new titles every month for just £2.10* each, postage and packing free. I understand that I am under no obligation to purchase any books and I may cancel or suspend my subscription at any time, but the free books and gift are mine to keep, whatever I decide.

6A6R

BLOCK CAPITALS PLEASE

Ms	Mrs	Miss	Mr	Initials

Surname

Address

Postcode

Offer closes 31st December 1996. We reserve the right to refuse an application. *Prices and terms subject to change without notice. Offer valid in UK and Ireland only and is not available to current subscribers to this series. Overseas readers please write for details. Southern Africa write to: IBS Private Bag X3010, Randburg 2125.

You may be mailed with offers from other reputable companies as a result of this application. If you would prefer not to share in this opportunity, please tick box.

The Reader Service
FREEPOST
Croydon
Surrey
CR9 3WZ

NO
STAMP
NEEDED

SEND NO MONEY NOW

in the quirk of his mouth that sent a tremor of apprehension through her.

'Is that so, Ms Brent? You know, that sounds uncommonly like a declaration of war to me. And I think it only fair to warn you that I'm a mean fighter.'

CHAPTER FIVE

ALISON'S feelings were still in turmoil when Rod dropped them off in the driveway of the townhouse. However, she was given little opportunity to ponder the exchange of hostilities which had just taken place. Rod said goodbye pleasantly enough, and drove off without any attempt to wangle an invitation to afternoon tea, although she had the uneasy suspicion that he was merely biding his time.

When she went inside, there was no chance of privacy either. Lyn was still there, ready for a drink and a chat after spending most of the day unpacking, and of course Cathy was still bursting with news about her first day at school. Even after Lyn had gone home, there was dinner to cook, a new school dress of Cathy's to be shortened, and bedtime, bathtime and a story to supervise.

It was nearly nine o'clock before Alison had the leisure to be alone and think her own thoughts.

Frowning thoughtfully, she slipped into her new bathing suit, still damp from its immersion in Rod's pool, and made her way outside to the luxurious spa bath adjacent to the swimming pool. It was a warm evening, with a velvety sky full of stars, and she had expected to find the area crowded, but to her relief all the other families seemed to be indoors watching television and she had the whole place to herself.

Draping her towel over the safety fence, she slipped into the hot, inviting water and turned on the bubbles. For a while she was content to lie in mindless bliss as the powerful jets of foaming water pummelled her body. But after a while the events of the day came creeping back to haunt her, and she switched off the bubbles and sat upright in the slowly subsiding turbulence. The underwater lights had come on in the swimming pool, so that it glowed like a turquoise gemstone, and ripples of light danced over the stems of the green shrubs planted near its edge.

A feeling of restlessness and dissatisfaction gripped her, in spite of the beauty of her surroundings. What disturbed her most was the knowledge that she and Cathy owed their presence here to Rod. She didn't want to owe him anything. It created a sense of obligation which warred violently with the antagonism she felt towards him.

If only she could be certain why he had brought her here! In spite of his glib explanations, she wasn't at all sure that he really needed her services as a driver. Filmmaking took months of forward planning, and she felt sure that Rod would be a very thorough planner. So had he only hired her in the hope of seducing her? If so, it seemed a very expensive operation!

Of course, Rod could easily afford the cost of her salary, but it didn't make sense. How could he be sure that his scheming would be rewarded? And anyway why go to so much trouble? There were heaps of better looking women than Alison already living in Noosa, who were single, childless and would probably jump at the chance of having a fling, however brief, with Rod Swift.

Or had he done it because he was so impressed by her talent and was determined to wear down her resistance to acting in his film? It was possible, but Alison doubted it—especially when so many other women were clamouring for the part. Or was he motivated by simple gratitude, because of her help after the accident?

Her lips curled sceptically at the mere thought. Somehow she didn't think the way Rod had kissed her in the swimming pool today had had anything to do with gratitude. Of course, there was always the possibility that he genuinely liked her, was genuinely attracted to her... But if that was so, where on earth did Marielle fit in?

In the end Alison gave up the puzzle in disgust. She would simply have to stick to the vow that she had made this afternoon—that the relationship between her and Rod was to be strictly business!

It was shortly before nine o'clock when she arrived at the Eumundi farmhouse the following morning, and the place was already buzzing with activity. Four large vans labelled 'Camera Crew', 'Wardrobe', 'Make-up' and 'Canteen' were already parked in an area of trampled grass next to a barn, and people were coming and going busily from all of them. Several actors in nineteenth-century costume were standing around with mugs of coffee and scripts in their hands.

Alison's features creased into a thoughtful frown as she climbed out of her vehicle and slammed the door. Now that she came to think about it, seven a.m. would have seemed a more reasonable starting time for her work rather than nine o'clock. Had Rod shown favouritism towards her because he knew she had to drop Cathy off at school? And wasn't it just one more sign that she wasn't really needed here? She would have to have the matter out with him! Although the present arrangement suited her ideally, she didn't want to have an unfair advantage over his other workers.

As she opened the front door of the farmhouse her

heart gave a skip of anticipation and she felt her breathing come faster, but there was no sign of Rod in the dining-room which had been converted into an office. The dark-haired production assistant called Kelly sat chewing gum and talking on the telephone. Catching sight of Alison, she transferred the wad of gum deftly to her left cheek.

'I'll be with you in a moment,' she mouthed.

Alison looked around her while she waited. The place was in chaos, with the only sign of order being a whiteboard fixed to one wall with everybody's name and timetable for the day jotted down in red felt-tipped pen. The desk was littered with scripts, white plastic coffee-cups, a photographic lamp, a coil of extension cord and an old-fashioned brass lantern.

Alison had just discovered that her own name was missing from the whiteboard when Kelly set down the phone, sniffed, blew a large pink bubble and grinned enquiringly at her.

'What can I do for you?'

'I've been hired as a driver. Rod brought me in to meet you the other day.'

To her annoyance she found that there was a tremor in her voice as she spoke his name, but Kelly didn't seem to notice.

'Oh, yes,' she said. 'Sorry. It's a real madhouse around here, and I'm not exactly sure what you're supposed to be doing. And Rod's not coming in today, so I can't ask him.'

Alison felt a pang of irrational disappointment at this news.

'Didn't he tell you what he wanted me to do?'

'No, he didn't,' replied Kelly with a shrug. 'Why don't you just hang around for a bit, and I'm sure somebody will have some good ideas?'

'But I don't want to sit just doing nothing,' protested Alison, feeling more useless and frustrated with every passing minute. Then she had a sudden inspiration. Hadn't Rod said something about Quentin and some shooting schedules yesterday? 'What about Quentin? Is he here? Couldn't he find me something to do?'

'Oh, I'm sure he can,' agreed Kelly with relief. 'Here he comes now. Quentin, have you met Alison? Rod's hired her as a gofer. Can you find her some jobs to do?'

Alison felt the same instinctive twinge of dislike that she had experienced on the day of the accident as Quentin came swinging through the doorway on crutches to greet her.

He looked as handsome as ever, especially when his eyes lit up at the sight of her. His left leg was in plaster and a small break in his luxuriant blond hair showed a rectangle of shaven skin and a neat row of stitches. Otherwise he seemed perfectly fit. At any rate he was fit enough to utter a theatrical cry of delight, and to set down his crutches and enfold Alison in a fervent hug.

'Darling, it's *won*derful to see you! It was amazing luck that you arrived on the scene so soon after our accident the other day. I'm enormously grateful to you.'

After the first euphoric crush Quentin did not release Alison, but merely slackened his hold slightly. Even so, she was aware of something unpleasantly suggestive in the grip of his fingers on her arm and in the way his gaze slid down her body. She was wearing one of her new outfits—a gauzy, emerald-green gathered skirt with a matching top—and she looked ten times better than she had on the day when she'd first met Quentin. All the same, she felt far more irritated than flattered when his expression changed from one of cool scrutiny to surprised approval.

'Perhaps I could take you out to dinner some time to thank you?' he added.

Alison's eyes flashed. Oh, so he's just decided that I'm pretty enough to be worth the cost of a dinner, has he? she thought with acid amusement. Her body stiffened, and she was about to step back a pace when she heard the creak of a floorboard in the doorway. Glancing up, she saw Rod framed in the doorway scowling fiercely at them. His jealousy and resentment were so obvious that she reacted without a moment's thought.

'Dinner, Quentin?' she murmured. 'I don't know how I'm placed this week, so I'll have to let you know, but it sounds lovely.'

'Quentin!' Rod's voice cut through the room like the crack of a whiplash. 'The cameramen are ready to begin filming the farmhouse scene. They'd like you on the set immediately.'

Quentin's eyes were cold and his mouth compressed as he picked up the crutches and limped to the door. The hostility between the two men was unmistakable, but after giving Rod a curt, unsmiling nod, Quentin winked at Alison as if there were some secret understanding between them, and vanished.

'Oh, Rod,' babbled Kelly, seeming totally unaware of the tension in the room. 'I didn't think you were coming in today.'

'I changed my mind,' said Rod in a surly voice. 'Are there any messages for me?'

'No. . . Yes! The actors from Melville Island are arriving this morning instead of tomorrow, and they want someone to pick them up from Maroochydore Airport at ten twenty-five.'

'You can do that,' ordered Rod curtly, turning to Alison. 'Not in the four-wheel drive, though. Take the blue minibus that's parked outside the barn.'

His disapproving scowl made her feel like a fifteen-year-old hauled up before the headmaster for kissing a boy behind the gym. With a defiant toss of her head, Alison edged her way to the door.

'What do I do with them when I get them?' she asked.

'Bring them here or take them to their hotel?'

Rod smiled at her. A grim smile, which sent tingles of unreasoning alarm up her spine.

'I'll give you instructions on the way.'

Alison stared at him in dismay.

'Does that mean you're coming too?'

'Yes, it'll give us a good opportunity to talk.'

There was nothing Alison could do to prevent him from coming with her, but she felt a powerful surge of misgiving as they walked down the narrow hall of the cottage together. From the first moment she had met Rod, she had sensed that he had a formidable temper beneath his urbane manner, and now she could see that he was spoiling for a fight.

Well, she would give him one and see how he liked it! It would be a pleasure to tell him what she thought of men with the mating habits of tomcats, constantly on the prowl for new partners! If he was involved with Marielle Mercer, as Alison still suspected in spite of his protests, what right did he have to try and ensnare other women?

They emerged on to the veranda and, almost as if Alison's thoughts had summoned her, Marielle detached herself from a pensive pose against the railing and glided across to them. She was wearing nineteenth-century costume and she looked so alluring that Alison's heart sank. Why couldn't she have a lush, creamy bosom like that, or wide, sensual lips? Marielle's dark eyes met hers, and Alison felt that she was looking at a deeply unhappy woman. There was no

mistaking the curiosity and resentment in Marielle's
face, or the stubborn determination to win, whatever
the cost.

After her piercing scrutiny of Alison, Marielle shifted
her gaze to Rod and she gave him a confident, almost
feline smile. Something in the way Marielle laid her
hand on Rod's arm and the impatient, but unsurprised
movement with which he shook it off, made Alison's
heart sink like a stone. There was no doubt in her mind
that a long familiarity existed between these two, even
if it was compounded largely of tension and mutual
reproach.

'I need to see you, Rod,' said Marielle hoarsely.
'There are things we must talk about. You don't really
need to go with Alison, do you?'

Rod scowled, and something about the harsh line of
his mouth gave Alison the unpleasant feeling that she
would not like to be in Marielle's shoes. When he
spoke, his voice was curt to the point of rudeness.

'Yes, I do need to go with Alison, but I can spare you
five minutes. Alison, go and wait for me in the minibus,
please.'

If he hadn't been her employer, she would have told
him to go to hell. As it was, she had no choice but to
walk down to the parking area and climb into the
vehicle.

It was too far away for her to hear what Marielle and
Rod were saying, and, in any case, she wouldn't have
eavesdropped. All the same, she couldn't help being
devoured by curiosity and resentment as she watched
them from a distance through the windscreen.

What a lot you could tell from body language! she
thought bitterly. Marielle seemed alternately haughty,
reproachful and flirtatious, and Rod looked exasperated and withdrawn. She had the distinct impression

that they were quarrelling about her, and her embar-
rassment and discomfort were only intensified when
Rod suddenly broke away from Marielle and came
striding down to the minibus with a face like thunder.
Climbing into the passenger side, he slammed the door.

'Right, let's go!' he ordered tersely.

Not a word of explanation. Nothing! In theory, it
might be none of Alison's business, but in practice she
was damned certain the argument had been about her.
So why didn't Rod explain anything? His next words
only fanned the flames of her annoyance.

'I'd like you to have dinner with me tonight.'

'Is this part of my job?'

'No.'

'Then, thanks, but no thanks. Even if I wanted to,
which I don't, I'll be otherwise occupied.'

'With Quentin, I suppose,' sneered Rod.

Alison's eyes glinted with rage. She had no intention
of having dinner with Quentin, but she wasn't going to
give Rod the satisfaction of telling him that.

'Why not?' she retorted coldly. 'At least he appears
to be on the unattached list.'

'Don't bet on it! As long as I've known Quentin, he's
always had at least two or three attachments on the go
at any one time—if you could call them that. They don't
last long, though, a few weeks at the most. You'd be a
fool to get involved with him. He's a total bastard when
it comes to women.'

'As opposed to you, who are heaven's gift to the
female sex, is that it?'

'I didn't say that!'

'It's just as well, because it wouldn't have sounded
very credible. If you ask me, you're the one who's an
absolute brute in your dealings with women.'

'And you're able to say that on the basis of a week's acquaintance?'

'No! I'm able to say it on the basis of watching you in action with Marielle—and don't give me that rubbish about how she's not your girlfriend! I can tell by looking at you that you've been involved with each other for ages. Haven't you? Haven't you?'

Rod caught his breath in a rasping gulp, as if he were in the world weight-lifting championships.

'No,' he grated.

Alison's only response was a raucous laugh in the back of her throat.

'All right, then. All right!' snapped Rod. 'We were involved. But it was a long time ago and it's finished—it's been finished for years.'

'She doesn't seem to think so!'

'That's her problem.'

'Oh, great! You're compassionate too when it comes to dumping people, are you? As well as truthful and sensitive and considerate?'

'For heaven's sake, Alison, it wasn't like that! Give me a chance and I'll explain it to you. Have dinner with me tonight.'

'No, I'm not interested in having dinner with you. I've got a daughter to spend my evenings with, in case you've forgotten. I don't have time for candlelit dinners with fly-by-night businessmen!'

She almost spat the words at him, and had to jam on the brakes as a tractor turned suddenly out of a farm lane on to the road in front of them. They both jerked forward and narrowly avoided hitting their heads on the windscreen. Rod took a long, shuddering breath and spoke as if he was controlling himself with great difficulty.

'Look, this is no place to argue. Of course you must

spend your evenings with Cathy, and I'd like to get to
know her better too. But you and I do need to talk.
What if we take Cathy out together on the weekend and
have dinner afterwards? Your sister-in-law could baby-
sit, couldn't she?'

'No,' purred Alison, skirting round the tractor which
was now rumbling peacefully down the centre of the
wide main street of Eumundi.

Rod gritted his teeth.

'There are some nice places we could go. We could
take her in a boat up to Lake Cooroibah, or we could go
down to the Gold Coast to one of the theme parks.'

'No,' repeated Alison sunnily, beginning to hum to
herself.

Rod swore under his breath.

'You're the most infuriating woman I've ever met.
But just wait—just wait! I'll deal with you yet.'

On Sunday morning at eight a.m. Alison and Cathy sat
enjoying their breakfast on the back patio overlooking
the garden. The croissant man had just driven away in
his van and Alison was in a pleasant stupor induced by
an early swim, two almond croissants and an excellent
cup of coffee.

It was too good to last. She had just opened up the
weekend newspaper and was lazily glancing at Cathy,
who was now turning cartwheels round the bed of
tropical vegetation in the centre of the lawn, when there
was a shrill squeal from her daughter.

'Cathy! Have you hurt yourself?' cried Alison, jumping up and spilling half her coffee.

'No, no!' called Cathy from behind the shrubs. 'But
look who's here, Mummy!'

The little girl emerged from behind the shrubs with
grass stains on her knees, leading a familiar figure by

the hand. It was a muscular, dark-haired man, dressed in navy shorts and a striped polo top, with an unfathomable expression in his grey eyes and a faint, lazy smile playing about the edges of his mouth.

'It's Rod,' announced Cathy unnecessarily.

'I can see that,' said Alison, with an edge to her voice. 'What are you doing here? Do you want me to work today?'

'No,' replied Rob, sinking uninvited into a plastic garden chair. 'I want you and Cathy to come to Sea World with me today. I think the outing would do us all good.'

There was a yell of rapture as Cathy launched herself at Rod and hugged him.

'Yes. Yes!' she cried. 'Please, please, Mummy, say we can go!'

A pang of resentment shot through Alison as she looked at the pair of them. Cathy's face was alight, her blue eyes dancing with glee, her lips parted in a joyful grin that displayed all the gaps in her teeth, and her freckled nose was wrinkled. Rod looked pleased with himself too. There was a hint of triumph in his smile that annoyed Alison unbearably.

'I suppose you think you're clever, outmanoeuvring me like that—asking me in front of Cathy because you think I can't say no. Well, I can!'

The brightness was suddenly extinguished from Cathy's face, as if a rain cloud had blotted out the sun. She looked at Alison with a hurt, bewildered expression.

'Does that mean we can't go, Mummy?' she faltered.

That was even worse. Now she felt like a monster, ruining her only child's happiness for no good reason. And when Rod's hand came up and patted Cathy's chubby paw reassuringly she felt worse still, as if they were in league against her. A gnawing sense of jealousy prickled inside her, although she also felt a twinge of shame at being so petty.

'I didn't say that,' she said shortly. 'I'll have to think about it. Go upstairs and wash that grass off your knees and put some clean clothes on while I talk to Rod.'

As Cathy scampered hopefully inside, shutting the screen door with a crash, Alison knew that she had already lost the battle. She stirred her cooling coffee and set the spoon down with a clatter.

'I wish you wouldn't do that!' she exclaimed. 'Getting her hopes up so that I look mean if I refuse. It's not fair.'

Rod had the grace to look ashamed.

'No,' he admitted with a grimace. 'You're right, it isn't really. I'm sorry.'

But by now Alison was thoroughly wound up, and his apology barely registered with her.

'It's not easy being a single parent,' she burst out.

'I know. I think you're doing a damned good job.'

'No, you don't! You think I'm an ogre who won't let my daughter have any fun.'

'That's not true, Alison!' he exclaimed impatiently. 'I think you're a very conscientious mother who needs a break herself now and again. I meant this trip to be fun for all of us, and I'm sure you'd enjoy it if you'd let yourself. You're too tense, too worried. I want to see you laugh; I want you to relax and be happy.'

He leaned forward in his chair, took her hand and gazed into her eyes with an intentness that made her heart race. Did he mean it? If so, it was the nicest thing that anyone had said to her in a long, long time. It made her feel so cherished, so safe, so full of bright hopes for the future. Yet if he didn't mean it, then it was the cruellest thing that anybody had ever said to her in a long, long time.

If Rod was only spinning her a line in order to persuade her to go to bed with him, then his strategy was diabolically clever. He must be well aware of the powerful physical attraction she felt towards him, but if the attraction were only physical, she would be running for cover by now. What made Rod so dangerous and so irresistible was that he seemed to be offering to meet all her other needs as well. Needs she had scarcely recognised in the past, but which were now awake and leaving her shaken with their hurricane-force intensity. The need for love, for companionship, for an affectionate father figure for her daughter, the need to escape from the past.

Yet there was so much holding her back. Not only the worrying question of whether Rod was involved with Marielle, but her own doubts and fears about commitment. After all she had been through, did she really want to take the risk of embarking on another relationship? And would Rod want her if he knew the truth?

Suddenly she felt a surge of revulsion against the secrecy, the concealment that had been going on for years. For one crazy moment she hovered on the brink of blurting out everything to Rod. But would he understand or would he simply despise her? She wasn't sure, and she no longer trusted her own power to judge.

Her body stiffened and she drew back. That small movement brought a flash of exasperation to Rod's eyes. Exasperation and something else. Something raw and urgent that sent a thrill of passion and desire throbbing through her, in spite of her qualms. Rod lifted his hand and trailed the edge of it down her cheek. She shuddered at his touch and instinctively moved closer, her lips parted.

'Are you kissing my mother?' demanded Cathy with interest, emerging from the house.

They sprang apart, Alison flushing crimson, Rod looking as unruffled as ever.

'No,' he said tranquilly. Yet as Alison shooed Cathy inside with orders about sunscreen, bathing gear and hair brushing he whispered in her ear. 'But I'd like to.'

Alison was busy with her own thoughts most of the way to the Gold Coast. Fortunately Rod seemed perfectly happy to listen to a jazz tape and watch the banana plantations and pineapple fields and stands of lush green sugar cane skim past. Cathy was quite good too, although once they'd passed the halfway point she began to demand plaintively, 'Are we there yet, Mummy?' every five minutes.

Alison was fervently grateful when the turreted entrance of Sea World came into view, with the mono-rail soaring high above the car park.

'What should we do first?' asked Rod as they passed into the entrance hall.

Cathy's eyes gleamed.

'Rides,' she begged. 'The Corkscrew and the Pirate Ship.'

Alison groaned. She suffered from mild vertigo, and the last thing she wanted after a two-hour drive was to be hurtled around at high speed on a roller coaster or swung backwards and forwards on a giant ship.

'How about the carousel?' she suggested cunningly. 'Or that nice little train?'

Cathy stuck her lip out.

'No, I want to go on the good rides—the ones that make you sick.'

'I'll take her,' offered Rod. 'You sit down and have some coffee or something.'

Feeling mildly guilty and hugely relieved, Alison allowed him to buy her a Coke and sat watching while the pair of them zoomed around at high speed. Her earlier resentment about being railroaded into this trip slowly melted away. It really was kind of Rod, she thought. I only hope he doesn't look too green when he comes off that thing! Fortunately Rod emerged from the roller coaster looking almost as delighted as Cathy.

'How about the whales, the dolphins and the sea lions next?' he suggested.

They all enjoyed the performing sea creatures, and the hot sun, the sparkling blue water and the antics of the animals began to work on Alison's spirits. She found herself relaxing and smiling broadly at the high points of the show. At the same time she was intensely aware of Rod's muscular body so close to hers on the wooden bench. Looking down at those powerful sun-tanned thighs, with their dusting of black hair, she felt a mysterious ache, a yearning to be alone with him. He caught her gaze and smiled at her.

For lunch they went to the hot dog hut. It was intended as a treat for Cathy, but Alison enjoyed it too. It was like a reversion to childhood to wolf down fat red frankfurters and soft white bread with mustard and tomato sauce dripping delectably onto her fingers. They filled the empty spaces with chocolate ice creams and Coke, and then went for a leisurely walk.

With a feeling of sheepish astonishment, Alison realised that she really was enjoying herself, although wild horses wouldn't have made her admit it to Rod.

'Can we go on the roller coaster again?' demanded Cathy.

'No,' said Rod firmly. 'It's your mother's turn to choose what we'll do now.'

Cathy opened her mouth to argue, intercepted Rod's

warning frown and closed it again. Why doesn't she take notice of me like that? wondered Alison with a twinge of envy. Perhaps it's because Rod's so strong and certain of himself. It gives her a feeling of security to know he's in control of the situation, even if she resents it. The humiliating thought flashed into her mind that her own reactions to Rod were remarkably similar.

'Well, what's your choice, Alison?' asked Rod.

'How about a ferry ride to digest our lunch and then a swim?'

A cool breeze and a shady canopy made the ferry ride a genuine pleasure, and Cathy was ecstatic when at last they came to the swimming pools and water slides.

'Can I go on the water slide?' she begged.

'No,' said Rod. 'Not until you can swim.'

'Will you teach me?'

'Yes.'

'Now?' she begged.

'If you like. We can have our first lesson, anyway.'

Alison opened her mouth to tell Cathy to stop being a nuisance, but Rod gripped her shoulder.

'It's OK,' he assured her. 'I'll take care of her. You can swim or have a rest.'

She did both. As she glided through the silky jade-green water the burdens of sole parenthood slipped off her shoulders, and she thought how much easier it was to enjoy a child when there was somebody else to share its care. After a long, refreshing swim she lay down on her towel on the grass and was dozing in the sun when Rod and Cathy came back and dripped water all over her. Rod seized her hand and pulled her into a sitting position.

'Why don't you go on the water slide?' he suggested.

Alison made a face.

'Because I'm too scared,' she admitted.

'But you'd like to?' he persisted.

'I suppose I would.'

'Then you've got to do it. I'll stay here with Cathy, to make sure she doesn't do anything dangerous, but I want you to climb that ladder and come down the water slide. Go on, I'll give you a count of five. One—'

Grumbling and hesitating, not even certain that he meant it, Alison began to walk towards the approach to the water slide. The fact that Cathy's eyes were wide with admiration and disbelief made it a little easier to put her foot on the bottom step.

'Look, I'm not sure—' she began.

'Two,' continued Rod relentlessly.

'I'm really a bit—'

'Three.'

'Oh, this is so silly! I can't!'

'Four.'

'If I get killed doing this, you'll be to blame.'

'Five.'

At the very moment he said it, she launched herself into space. There was an exhilarating sense of panic and speed, a great swoosh of flying spray, then she hit the water at the bottom with a resounding smack, felt bubbles explode all around her and came up laughing and gasping, filled with exhilaration and triumph.

'I did it! I really did it!' she gabbled as she came hurrying back across the grass towards them. 'I can't believe it! I didn't think I'd have the courage.'

'You've got enough courage for anything,' said Rod approvingly, draping her towel around her shoulders and gripping it in front of her as if she were a Christmas parcel that needed further wrapping. 'All you have to do is stop listening to your fears and let go. It's safer than it looks.'

'Stop listening to your fears and let go'. If she used that as her motto in this relationship, where would she end up? Was it safer than it looked? Could she trust Rod to take care of her? Gazing up into his narrowed grey eyes, she took in breath in a sudden, shuddering gulp. You could mean so much to me, she thought apprehensively. But I'm frightened of just plunging in. . .

There was another poignant moment as they were getting ready to go home. Their last call was at the gift shop, where Rod bought Cathy a fluffy white toy seal. As he was drawing out his wallet to pay for it his keys dropped unnoticed to the floor. Another customer picked them up and handed them to Cathy.

'Tell your daddy he's just dropped his keys,' said the woman kindly.

Cathy tugged on Rod's arm and handed him the keys.

'That lady thought you were my daddy,' she announced, and then gave a fervent sigh. 'I wish you were!'

Cathy fell asleep on the long drive home, and did not stir even when Rod carried her up to bed and removed her sandals. He stood for a moment, looking down at the sleeping child with an expression of such amusement on his face that Alison felt a renewed rush of affection for him.

'Will you come out to dinner with me?' he whispered as they tiptoed away.

'I can't,' she said, halting halfway down the stairs. 'I can't leave Cathy.'

Another man might have grown impatient, but Rod's voice remained mild and reasonable.

'Don't forget there's a babysitting service here,' he reminded her. 'The tourists use it all the time. All you have to do is lift the telephone and call the manager's office. They have some very reliable girls who come in at a moment's notice.'

'But she might wake and be alarmed if she finds a stranger here.'

'We'll leave the restaurant phone number with the babysitter, and we'll come home immediately if she gets upset,' replied Rod patiently.

Alison pulled a wry face as she realised that she had run out of excuses. Then, with a stirring of surprise, she realised something else. That she really did want to go out to dinner with Rod.

'All right,' she agreed, to her own amazement. 'I'll come.'

Even Rod looked a shade taken aback, but he was swift to follow up his advantage.

'I'll pick you up in an hour,' he promised.

Once he had left, Alison took a long, leisurely shower, then dressed in one of the new outfits she had bought in Hastings St. It was a silky metallic-blue trouser suit, so gossamer-thin that it seemed weightless, which draped into graceful folds when she moved. Once she was dressed she did her make-up carefully and stared at herself in the large bathroom mirror.

She was surprised by the look of luminous excitement in her face. Her eyes looked huge and soft, and there was a wistful curve to her lips. She felt both much younger and much older—filled with the confidence of youth, but also strengthened by experience. The eternal woman, she thought to herself, half mockingly.

Suddenly she heard soft, padding footsteps, and a small figure clutching a white toy seal materialised beside her.

'You look pretty, Mummy. Where are you going?'

Alison crouched down and opened her arms for a big hug.

'Rod invited me out to dinner,' she said. 'But I don't have to—'

'That's nice. I hope you have a good time. Who's minding me? Auntie Lyn?'

'No, a babysitter.'

'Great! I bet she'll let me watch TV till midnight.'

Alison laughed, and tweaked her daughter's nose.

Not long afterwards Rod arrived to fetch her, just as he had promised. Like her, he had obviously taken trouble over his grooming. He was wearing beige trousers, a pale blue shirt and a well-cut navy sports-coat, and he carried a single, long-stemmed red rose. He bent and kissed Alison's cheek, and she knew from the smoothness of his skin and the spicy whiff of cologne that he had just finished shaving. A rush of gratitude and excitement flared through her as he handed her the rose.

'For me? Thank you! It's beautiful. I'll just put it in water before we go.'

They said goodbye to Cathy and the babysitter and left the house.

'Do you feel like walking to the restaurant?' asked Rod. 'It's only a couple of blocks away, and there's a magnificent full moon over the river.'

He was right. The tropical night settled around them like a dark velvet cloak as they walked down the driveway between the clumps of softly lit bushes and flowering plants. Emerging into the street, they found a huge frangipani bush looming above them, its pale blooms glowing like lamps and sending out a rush of intoxicatingly sweet fragrance.

Rod took her hand to guide her along the uneven grassy footpath and a thrill of pride and pleasure tingled through Alison's veins at the warm, strong clasp of his fingers on hers. I'm happy, she thought with a touch of awe. I've never been so happy in my life before.

She walked in silence, her senses alert to every detail, wanting to imprint this moment on her memory for ever. The croaking of frogs, the whir of unseen insects, the golden radiance of the moon shining through the trees ahead and illuminating the dark river all seemed a part of an extraordinary symphony of happiness that was swirling like glorious music inside her.

The noise from the restaurant hit them when they were still twenty metres away from it, a cheerful uproar of laughter and music and clinking glasses. Alison's spirits sank slightly. Although she was feeling happy, it was a quiet, reflective happiness, and she would have preferred a quiet corner to a crowded room. Yet when the proprietor came threading his way through the densely packed tables and laughing, chattering guests, her prayer was unexpectedly answered.

'Good evening, Mr Swift, good evening, madam. We've got a family party here tonight, celebrating a twenty-fifth wedding anniversary, so I've put you in the small private dining-room upstairs. I hope that will suit you.'

He led the way up the narrow wooden stairs and opened the door of a small room overlooking the river. Alison gave a soft exclamation of delight as she saw the candlelight flickering on the buttercup-yellow walls and reflecting off the blue glassware on the table. The table itself was set next to the large, uncurtained window overlooking the moonlit river and was covered with a yellow and white striped tablecloth and set with Italian maiolica plates. The three remaining tables in the room were all empty.

With a deft movement the restaurateur pulled out a comfortably padded cane chair for Alison and shook a yellow and white striped napkin over her lap. Then he repeated the same service for Rod.

'I'll leave you to look at the drinks menu, Mr Swift, and I'll be back shortly to take your order.'

The door closed behind him and a moment later a nostalgic Italian song swirled into the air from a hidden speaker behind a pot plant.

'Is this all right?' asked Rod. 'Or would you prefer a bit more company?'

Alison shook her head.

'It's perfect,' she assured him.

Before long they were sipping drinks—Scotch on the rocks for Rod and a bittersweet Italian aperitif for Alison—and arguing amiably over the best things to eat. In the end they agreed to share an antipasto followed by chicken cacciatore with fried potatoes and salad for Alison and a large beefsteak in wine sauce for Rod. The service was swift and unobtrusive, and soon they were eating delicious sun-dried tomatoes, prosciutto, tender pickled vegetables and rounds of bland white cheese.

Alison gave a sigh of contentment as she finally set her knife and fork side by side on her plate.

'Have another one,' suggested Rod.

'No, thanks. I'm saving myself for the main course, and after that I'm going to have one of those delicious Italian gelati, if I can manage it. Cathy would die of envy if she knew.'

'She seemed to settle down all right, didn't she?' asked Rod.

Alison gave a rueful laugh.

'Yes, she did. As a matter of fact I think she was pleased to get rid of me.'

There was a touch of regret in her voice.

'Well, she won't be your baby for ever,' said Rod

wisely. 'She's going to grow up and want a life of her own, and it's only fair that you should have the same.'

'I suppose so,' agreed Alison. 'It seems a bit sad, though. She means the world to me.'

'Would you ever want to have another child?' he demanded unexpectedly.

The question was so abrupt and so full of hidden meanings that it took her by surprise. She blushed violently as she thought of the implications. Love, marriage, a man permanently in her life. But perhaps it didn't mean any of those things to Rod? Perhaps he thought she would blithely become pregnant by someone she hardly knew and then bring up another child alone?

Her lip curled scornfully. After six years of shouldering the loneliness and heartache of single parenthood, she would never, never do that! Although, she reflected, her years of shouldering the loneliness and heartache of marriage didn't make that very appealing either. And yet Rod's question had touched off a chain reaction of complicated longings inside her.

Darting a troubled glance at his rugged, intense features she felt an arrow of yearning pierce her. Yearning to love and be loved, to have another baby as a culmination of shared passion and commitment. Of course, she could not possibly tell him any of this. It was too deep, too private. Besides, she had only known him for such a short time.

'You have a very expressive face,' he said softly, reaching out his hand and touching hers. 'I can see so much there. Anger, bitterness, exhaustion. And yet I can see other things there too. Warmth, longing, a desire for commitment. But you're still afraid, aren't you, Alison? Too afraid even to share your thoughts with me.'

She took a long, unsteady breath.

'Do you read minds?' she asked in a tormented voice.

'No. Only faces. But I'm right, aren't I? Tell me.'

'Yes!' she burst out. 'Although I don't know what business it is of yours. I do want to have another child, but after what I've been through, the thought appals me in some ways.'

'What have you been through?' he asked softly.

The familiar, cold feeling gripped her stomach like an icy hand. She stared blindly out at the moonlit river, willing herself not to dissolve into tears. In a moment the feeling would pass. But this time the strain of silence proved too great. To her horror she heard the words come spilling out.

'My husband was a drug addict, with all that that entails. His addiction made my life hell. Pure hell. He stopped showing up for work, he spent all our money on drugs and he began sleeping with women he met at drugs parties. I tried to reason with him, to beg him to stop. That was when the violence started.'

She heard Rod's sharp intake of breath and felt his hand clench on hers.

'He hit you?'

She nodded, her face strained and wretched.

'Why didn't you leave him?'

'I did.'

'And this was. . .how long after you were married?'

'A year.'

His features creased into a puzzled frown.

'What about your child? Had you already had her?'

'No. Cathy was born two years after that.'

'I don't see—'

'Harley came after me. He. . .raped me.'

She couldn't suppress the shudder that began as a cold tremor in the pit of her stomach and spread through her entire body. With a tiny, involuntary whimper she drew her hand out of his and sat back in her chair, pressing her clenched fist against her lips.

'The bastard,' Rod said thickly. 'It's a good thing he's dead. Otherwise I'd kill him for treating you like that.'

A spasm of distress crossed her face, then she shrugged and gave him a wan smile.

'Well, it's all over now,' she said, with an attempt at jauntiness.

'Like hell it is! I've known from the first moment I met you that some terrible pain was ripping you apart. The past is still well and truly alive for you, Alison, and it's poisoning your present. All the same, I'm glad you found the courage to tell me. Now that I know everything, I really hope I can help you get over it.'

'Now that I know everything'. The words echoed mockingly in Alison's head. Rod didn't know everything, not by a long shot. The most painful detail of all, the one that still gave her nightmares, was still a secret. For an instant she was tempted to tell him, to clear this last fence and have it over with, but then Rod spoke again and the moment was lost.

'You've done a wonderful job with Cathy,' he remarked, looking at her compassionately. 'You must have felt very frightened and resentful when you realised you were pregnant.'

'I did. I even used to fear that I could never love the baby, that it would always remind me... But, thank heaven, it wasn't like that! From the first moment I saw her, she was unbelievably precious to me.'

She realised that she was clenching and unclenching her hands in her agitation. With a conscious effort she set them down motionless on the tablecloth on either side of her plate.

'If you were choosing the circumstances to have

another child, how would you want it to be?' Rod asked thoughtfully. 'Would you do it alone?'

'No!' The reply was so vehement that he raised his eyebrows. Alison lowered her voice and continued in a rapid rush. 'I think that's wrong—unfair to everybody concerned. I believe in commitment, lasting relationships, love. I think people need that. I know I'm not a really shining example of how to do it, but that's what I'd want before I'd even contemplate having another child.'

'I see.' He lowered his glass and continued to regard her appraisingly. 'You interest me considerably.'

His measured tone touched Alison on the raw. Suddenly she felt outraged at the way he had led her into disclosing all these intimate details about her own feelings, while remaining totally aloof himself.

'And you annoy me considerably!' she retorted. 'You're so clinical, aren't you? You probe and dissect and analyse, you ask me anything you damn well like, no matter how private, and you give nothing in return. What about you? Don't you have any feelings behind that expressionless mask?'

He leaned forward and caught her by the hand, and suddenly his face was far from expressionless. His grey eyes kindled, the long creases appeared in his cheeks and his mouth twisted in a stormy line. Alison's heart began to thud wildly as she saw how he looked at her.

'Yes, I have feelings,' he replied hoarsely. 'Feelings every bit as deep as yours. And what I'm feeling at the moment is that I'd give everything I possess to have you naked in my bed. I'd make violent love to you all night long, and, if my deepest wishes were granted, I'd give you a child.'

CHAPTER SIX

She was saved from having to comment by the arrival of the waiter, who whisked away their empty plates and returned with their main courses. Alison felt deeply perturbed as she waited for him to leave the room. She was profoundly shocked by Rod's emphatic statement, but it also sent a rush of treacherous excitement throbbing through her.

His explicit admission that he wanted to make love to her and plant his child inside her made her go hot and cold with confusion. Worse still, it unleashed a raw, primal need that sent alarming erotic images rioting in her mind. She was honest enough to admit, at least to herself, that she felt an aching desire to make love with Rod. She imagined the slick hot power of his manhood thrusting deep within her. . .herself clinging to him. . . straining, gasping, crying out in fulfilment. . .

The waiter vanished from the room and Rod picked up his knife and fork. Without taking his eyes off her, he began methodically to attack his steak. Not knowing where to look, Alison dropped her eyes and groped for her own cutlery. In a dazed fashion she cut a piece of chicken and put it in her mouth. It was tender, aromatic, meltingly delicious, but she scarcely tasted it.

'You're quiet,' remarked Rod, as if they had been discussing nothing more dangerous than films or gardening.

Alison shot him a burning look. She was so agitated that her hand trembled as she picked up her glass of wine. The Chianti didn't help either. Its fresh, slightly prickly potency seemed to flow dangerously into her veins like fire, making her feel reckless and quite unlike herself.

'What can I say?' she muttered. 'It's outrageous of you even to mention such things.'

'Outrageous to tell the truth? It is the truth, you know, Alison.'

She set down the wine glass and poured herself some water instead. The carafe clinked against her tumbler, and the cool freshness of the water sobered her slightly.

'I don't even know what you mean by it,' she said unsteadily.

'I mean exactly what I said.'

She bit her lip and looked around the room, moving her head in a series of nervous, jerky movements. Did he mean that he wanted to go to bed with her? Well, that was simple enough, and not very surprising. There had been other occasions when men had made similar propositions to her, and she had fended them off without suffering a moment's disquiet. It was the second half of Rod's statement that really disturbed her. Nobody had ever told her that he wanted to give her a baby before, not even her husband. But what did Rod mean by it?

He couldn't possibly mean that he had fallen in love with her and wanted to marry her, since they had known each other for scarcely more than a week. So was he one of those men who delighted in trying to father as many offspring as they possibly could, with no real concern for the women involved? She had met several of them in Hollywood, all with a string of ex-wives and girlfriends abandoned along with their children. They infuriated her.

'Then you've no business to say it!' she flared. 'You don't even know me properly and you can't possibly know whether you'd want to have children with me. If you're going to talk like that, I'm leaving!'

She was already halfway out of her seat when he caught her wrist and hauled her back down.

'What's wrong?' he demanded.

'Everything!' she retorted. 'I don't like men whose one ambition is to populate the entire planet. I've met them before—mostly actors, with hordes of ex-wives and children and absolutely no commitment to any of them. If you ask me, they're just on an ego trip!'

'But I'm not like that,' growled Rod. 'All of this is a completely new experience to me. Wanting a child is something I never thought about much in the past, but since I've met you it seems very important. I don't know what you've done to me, but you've caused a complete upheaval in my thinking. I've never felt like this about another woman.'

Alison looked at him suspiciously. She wanted to believe him, but she was still tormented by doubt.

'What about Marielle?'

Rod grimaced and reached for his wine glass. He swirled the Chianti in his mouth, then winced as if he were swallowing medicine.

'I didn't want to talk about that, but I suppose I must. I never felt anything like that for Marielle, and I'm quite certain she never wanted it. We did have a relationship in the past, but it was a very long time ago and both of us soon decided that it was a complete mistake. I hadn't seen her much for years until Quentin cast her in this film.'

'Then why did she seem so upset at the thought that you were kissing me?'

'I can only put it down to vanity on her part,' he said with a shrug. 'Marielle has her good points, but she has an obsessive need for attention. In fact, she wants every man she meets to be her devoted slave for life, and it infuriates her that I won't play her little game. I don't want to seem unkind, but I'll be very relieved if I never have to set eyes on her again once this film is over.'

Alison was silent, pondering on what he had just told her. It seemed likely enough, especially after her own experiences in the film world. While many actresses were warm, sincere and selfless, there also seemed to be a huge number who craved constant adulation and flattery. If what Rod said was true, he probably deserved to be pitied rather than blamed. On the other hand, was he just trying to lull her suspicions so that she could be next on his list of conquests?

'Is this true?' she burst out.

'Yes, I swear it.' His voice rang with sincerity. Leaning forward, he took her hand and gazed at her with a stormy expression. 'I wouldn't lie to you, Alison. Whatever faults I may have, I'm essentially honest. Besides, you've become very important to me.'

A warm, tremulous feeling fluttered in her midriff and her hand leapt convulsively in his. Did he mean it?

'How can I be?' she protested. 'You've known me such a short time.'

'That doesn't matter! I've learnt to sum up people very quickly. Don't forget that I've been on climbing expeditions and exploring parties in remote areas. In those circumstances the veneer of civilisation is very quickly stripped away, and you soon learn to judge what you really feel towards people. And my feelings towards you are very, very powerful.'

Alison snatched herself free of his grip and looked down at the table with a shudder. What did that mean? It could mean anything, couldn't it? It could just mean that Rod had a very powerful urge to strip her clothes off as fast as possible. She shot him an appraising look.

'What do you want from me?' she demanded.

Something kindled in his eyes that made an alarming heat pulsate through her veins.

'I think you know that, don't you?' he said huskily. 'But I can see I'm moving too fast for you. I'm not a patient man by nature, but I'll try to curb my haste. Just don't shut me out, Alison. Keep seeing me and let us get to know each other. That's all I want from you. For now.'

He put out his hand to her invitingly, and she felt as if she were being coaxed onto a flimsy suspension bridge poised dizzily above a foaming cataract filled with saw-toothed boulders. She hesitated, eyeing him warily.

'Supposing I do, you won't make any more embarrassing declarations, will you?'

'No.'

'You won't try to kiss me. . .or. . .or. . .'

'I'm not going to make promises I can't keep! I fully intend to try and "kiss you. . .or. . .or. . .", but I think you're capable of letting me know if that's unwelcome. If it is, I'll stop. Reluctantly.'

Alison gave a sudden croak of laughter.

'You're so blatant!' she protested.

'No. Just honest about what I want. Well, will you do it? Will you let me see you on weekends, and take you and Cathy out? Will you take a chance on me?'

Alison sighed and then surrendered.

'Yes,' she said, placing her hand in his.

In the days that followed, she sometimes thought that that was the most exhilarating decision she had ever made in her life. She found herself almost constantly in Rob's company, and discovered that his presence was dangerously addictive. She had a shrewd suspicion that Rod didn't normally spend every single day on the set of other films he was backing, but she didn't cross-examine him about his presence. It was enough that he was there.

Her heart gave a little skip each time she glimpsed his muscular, athletic figure striding across to the farmhouse in the morning, or saw his harsh features light up at the sight of her at coffee-breaks. She didn't know where all this was leading, and she didn't dare to speculate. She simply felt a dizzy sense of excitement and pleasure in being with him.

For the first few days they had plenty of leisure to slip away from the rest of the filmmakers and simply stroll and talk among the green hills above the farmhouse. After that the whole crew went on location to Fraser Island, and Alison found herself really earning her salary.

Although the other vans were all equipped with four-wheel drive, she was by far the most experienced of the drivers, and was always the person called upon if a vehicle became bogged or any other problems occurred. On these occasions Rod was always the first to come to her aid, and she soon developed a deep respect for his stamina and ingenuity. They also found a shared satisfaction in taking nature walks and making the campsite as comfortable as possible.

However, Alison was careful to keep their dealings on a businesslike basis. Even though she believed his explanation about Marielle, she thought it tactless to flaunt their growing involvement in front of the other woman. Not that Marielle seemed likely to notice in any case. By now she was totally wrapped up in the character she was playing, and only seemed to become aware of other people if they were directly serving her or obstructing her in some way.

Alison found her behaviour fascinating. She could

pass from radiant smiles to prima donna tantrums in the blink of an eye. And now that Alison was observing her closely she saw evidence that Rod's accusation was true. Marielle did seem to have an obsessive craving for attention. Whenever there was an actor or cameraman nearby, she always needed a favour done. Some insect repellent or a glass of chilled orange juice or—seductive fluttering of luxuriant dark eyelashes—'just a few moments hearing my lines'.

Her favourite target in these manoeuvres was generally Quentin, and Alison was intrigued by the question of whether anything serious was going on between them. On one occasion she was rather inclined to think that there was.

Hurrying away from the campfire one night, to fetch a handkerchief from her tent, she almost cannoned straight into their dark shapes on the steps of Marielle's camper van. For a moment she could have sworn that they were kissing passionately, but at her muttered apology Quentin only laughed.

'Are you any good at mending insect screens?' he drawled. 'This wire door of Marielle's has a great gaping hole in it, and we've just been trying to fix it.'

Alison blinked and decided she was mistaken. The incident slipped from her mind, and it wasn't until much later that she realised it might be important. In any case, she was far too preoccupied with her own love life to worry much about Quentin or Marielle.

After the film crew's return from Fraser Island, the days flew past in a way that was almost miraculous.

Alison spent every weekend with Rod. Usually on one day they went on some kind of family outing with Cathy—picnics at Lake Cooroibah, swimming at Laguna Beach, bushwalking in the National Park—yet

Rod was quite ruthless in reserving some part of every weekend to be alone with Alison.

There were dinners in quiet little restaurants, noisy jazz concerts, a nostalgic trip to the old-fashioned cinema at Pomona, complete with Rudolf Valentino flicks and live organ playing. Most dangerous of all, there were evenings spent alone together in Rod's house on the sound.

He always stuck scrupulously to his bargain and, although there were kisses, he never tried to coax Alison further when she called a halt. The trouble was that as the end of filming approached she was miserably certain that she was falling in love with Rod. And she was no longer certain that she even wanted to call a halt.

Perhaps matters might have remained unresolved if she hadn't lost her favourite ring one day. She was loading the dishwasher after dinner when she discovered the loss.

'Cathy,' she called to her daughter. 'Have you seen Mummy's ring? The gold and amethyst one that Granny gave me for my birthday last year?'

Cathy turned reluctantly away from the television.

'No, Mummy. Maybe you left it at work or at Auntie Lyn's.'

Alison phoned her sister-in-law and drew a blank.

'Why don't you drive out to Eumundi and check?' suggested Lyn. 'You can leave Cathy here for the night.'

'All right. Thanks.'

Leaving a message with the manager, in case Rod phoned to find out where she was, Alison drove back to the farmhouse. It seemed rather eerie and deserted, with the moonlight casting inky shadows behind the barn and frogs croaking in the unseen reeds of the pond. Fumbling for her keys, she unlocked the door, switched on the light and went inside. Luckily she found the ring at once, on the washbasin in the bathroom.

Slipping it onto her finger, she came out again and was just about to leave when she saw that the costume intended for Charlotte was hanging on a rack in the converted living-room. On impulse she picked it up and held it against her in front of the full-length mirror on the wall. Her reflection stared back at her, dramatically altered by the drab grey gown, but still incongruous with the long, loose twentieth-century hairstyle. Wasn't there a wig somewhere that went with the costume?

Then she saw the candy-striped box directly beneath the rack. Without consciously pausing to think, she stripped off her own clothes and flung them down. Taking the dress off the hanger, she hauled it over her head and fastened it, her fingers fumbling on the unfamiliar hooks and eyes. After that she picked up the wig and put it on her head, tucking her own hair out of sight.

The transformation was dramatic. She looked like a completely different woman. An embittered, nineteenth-century spinster who still carried deep in her heart a passion for living and a gruff sympathy for another woman in trouble. She looked like Charlotte.

'I could play that part,' she said aloud. 'In fact, I could probably do it better than any of those four girls Quentin has shortlisted for it. They don't make her powerful or angry enough.'

Pondering for a moment, she thought of the scene she had heard one of the aspiring actresses read at her audition only that morning. The scene where Charlotte tried to persuade Eliza Fraser to let go of her harrowing past.

A dreamy, thoughtful expression came over her face. This electric light was too harsh—lamplight would be much better, and the brass lantern was right there on the table. It was a ridiculous self-indulgence, but what harm could it do? Shaking her head at her own absurdity, she found matches and lit the lantern. Then she switched off the overhead light and began to act.

'Forgive me if I'm intruding upon you, Mrs Fraser, but there's something I feel I must say. Ever since you came out of the wilderness and took shelter with us, I've known there was some unhappy secret that troubled you, and now I believe I've guessed what it is. You've fallen in love with another man after your husband's death, haven't you?

'Oh, pray, don't turn away, Mrs Fraser. Your secret is safe with me. Indeed, it is! And, if I may be permitted to advise you, I should urge you most earnestly to follow your heart. It is not your fault that Captain Fraser perished. You must not waste the rest of your life in senseless guilt for something you could not prevent!'

The echo of the tragedy in her own life gave Alison's voice an added resonance and urgency. As she came to the end of the words she caught her breath on a small half-sob and bowed her head. She was so absorbed that it came as an alarming surprise when the sound of clapping suddenly exploded into the room. With a gasp, she turned round.

'Quentin! You scared the life out of me. What are you doing here?'

'I saw the light and came to investigate. I had no idea you could act like that, Alison. I'll tell you right now that the part of Charlotte is yours. And, what's more, I'll make you my leading lady in my next film. You and I could go places together, baby.'

Was his voice slightly slurred, or was it her imagination? A brief flicker of misgiving went through her as she glanced up at his hazy blue eyes and the knowing smile that was curving the edges of his lips. She stepped back a pace.

'No, Quentin, I don't want the part, thanks. I was only fooling around. I'm just a driver.'

He took a step closer, the metal support under his plaster clanking on the floor.

'That's garbage,' he murmured, seizing her arms. His breath fanned her face and she caught the unmistakable whiff of some pungent liqueur. Drambuie, perhaps, or Cointreau? 'You're an actress and an exsheptionally talented one. It's time I had a few words alone with you. What about that dinner you promised me?'

'I don't think so, Quentin,' said Alison, pulling free. 'I'm sorry.'

'Why not?' demanded Quentin aggressively. 'You were keen enough before, but I suppose you're having it off with Rod now, aren't you? I've seen the way he looks at you, but you're wasting yourself on him. What you need is a bit of variety, Alison.'

With a sudden lunge he grabbed her again, almost overbalancing, and his mouth came down on hers, hot and moist and smelling of alcohol.

'You pig! Let me go!'

He was surprisingly strong, and Alison felt the first real twinge of fear as they grappled noisily together. Then suddenly the front door burst open with a sound like a pistol-shot and Rod loomed above them. He took in the situation at a glance, and with a low growl of anger hauled Quentin off Alison by the collar of his shirt.

'You scum!' he hissed. 'It's lucky for you you've got a plaster on your leg, or I'd knock you flat. Well, I'll just say this to you, you bastard. If you lay a finger on Alison again, I'll not only break every bone in your body, I'll also withdraw my money from the film. Now get out!'

Quentin stood glaring aggressively at both of them for a moment, then dropped his eyes and lurched towards the front door, swearing under his breath. The door crashed violently behind him and there was the sound of uneven footsteps staggering away.

'Do you think he'll make it safely to his cottage?' asked Alison.

It was Rod's turn to swear under his breath.

'Well, I for one don't care if he falls into the duck pond on his way!' he retorted savagely. 'Never mind that. Did he hurt you?'

Alison shook her head, but at that very moment reaction set in and she began to tremble. Rod hauled her into his arms and pressed his face into her hair. As he did so he gave an exclamation of surprise.

'What's this?' he asked, holding her at arm's length.

'A wig,' she replied, pulling it off hastily. 'I was—'

'You were trying on Charlotte's costume. Which means you're still interested in the part, doesn't it?'

'No, I—'

'Put it on again and read some of the lines to me.'

'No. I don't—'

'You know, it's the strangest thing, but with that dark hair, you looked like a completely different person. And I have the uncanny feeling that I know you. Wait, I'll put it back on.'

She flung up her hands to stop him, but it was too late. As the dark wig pressed down over her scalp a look of intent concentration kindled in Rod's eyes. She endured his scrutiny in silence, clenching her hands so hard that the nails dug into her palms. Her heart was beating in a frantic, unnatural rhythm, and her feelings were in turmoil for fear he would uncover the truth.

The truth. She flinched at the thought. Yet in a strange way, after morbidly dreading this moment for so many years, she felt almost relieved now that it was upon her. If Rod Swift was determined to drag it out of her, then let him! In any case, there was little she could do to stop him. He was pacing around now, firing a salvo of rapid, staccato questions at her.

'I've got it! Didn't you play the leading role in that film Rhett Barton made nine or ten years ago? The one about the nurse in wartime Sydney? But you weren't calling yourself Alison Brent then, were you? Now let me think, what was your name? Lana? Lara? I've got it—Lara Blythe!'

His grey eyes were blazing with triumph and certainty, so that Alison realised it was absolutely useless to deny it. She gave a small, defeated sigh.

'Lara Blythe,' she agreed. 'A silly name, really, but the director chose it. I think he had visions of presenting me as someone like the heroine of *Dr Zhivago*.'

'But you were!' insisted Rod. 'I'd never seen such powerful acting before from someone so young. You couldn't have been more than—what—twenty? Twenty-one?'

'Nineteen,' murmured Alison with a touch of pride.

Rod whistled.

'As young as that? Well, I can tell you, you stole the show from that piece of blond beefcake who played the Coral Sea fighter pilot. He was so wooden it was embarrassing. But there's no justice in this world. He went on to become a Hollywood megastar while you dropped out of sight completely. What happened? Why didn't you continue with your career? I would have thought directors would have been beating a path to your door, with contracts clutched in their hot little hands.'

Alison's lips twisted wryly.

'They were! But I fell in love and got married and my husband wouldn't let me do any more acting. He said I'd be away too much and the separations would destroy our relationship.'

'The selfish bastard!' exclaimed Rod. 'He had absolutely no right to stand in the way of a unique talent like yours. Why did you let him do it? Why did you agree to something so outrageous?'

'He wouldn't have married me otherwise. That was the condition he made when he proposed to me—that I had to give up my acting career and just be his wife.'

Rod gave a hoot of incredulous laughter.

'And you agreed? Didn't the acting mean anything to you?'

Alison felt a flare of annoyance at his ridicule.

'Of course it did! It meant a hell of a lot to me. You might not believe it to look at me now, but I used to love performing for an audience. I was quite outgoing when I was a teenager, and I was over the moon when I got my first part in a soapie. And then to have the leading role in a film—I felt as if I were walking on air! I would gladly have gone on acting for the rest of my life.'

'So why didn't you?'

'It wasn't that simple! I loved Harley; I thought I was doing the right thing.'

Rod looked startled.

'Harley? You mean, you married Harley Winchester? The blond beefcake who played the fighter pilot in that film?'

'Yes.'

'Then that means—'

He stopped dead in his tracks with a look of shocked comprehension. It was the moment Alison had dreaded. Her stomach contracted into a cold knot and she wished a chasm would open in the floor and swallow her. Snatching off the wig and flinging it away as if it were soaked in poison, she met his gaze despairingly.

'Yes. It means I killed my husband.'

'What? That's impossible!'

'Well, that's what the tabloids said, didn't they?' she exclaimed fiercely. 'And they couldn't possibly be wrong, could they? In any case, I'm not so sure that they were all that far off the truth!'

Her voice broke suddenly, and, dropping her head into her hands, she began to sob. Dreadful, wrenching sobs that threatened to tear her apart. Through the fog of misery that enveloped her, she felt Rod haul her roughly into his arms. He buried his face in her hair and held her until her sobs subsided.

'Suppose you tell me what really happened?' he growled, producing a handkerchief from his pocket and scrubbing her face.

'It was in Hollywood. . .about a year. . .after Cathy was born,' she choked. 'As you know, we were already separated, but Harley came to the house in the middle of the night and started knocking and shouting at the door. I was afraid he'd disturb the neighbours, so I let him in.'

'That was a mistake,' observed Rod drily.

'Yes, it was! As soon as I saw him, I realised he'd just had a hit. His eyes were bright and unfocused. He began to talk wildly about how he loved me and wanted me back. I told him our marriage was over. . .and he began to punch me. I ran upstairs and locked myself in Cathy's room and screamed at him through the window. I said terrible things, Rod. I said he was a hopeless father and a dreadful husband and I wished he was dead. I told him if he didn't leave I'd call the police.'

'And then?' Rod's voice was gentle, but implacable.

'And then he said. . .he said. . .if that was the way I felt, he'd go and kill himself.'

'So what happened then?'

'I heard his car start up and roar down the drive. I ran out to try and stop him, but he was gone. About four hours later I had a visit from a policeman who told me Harley had driven his car over a cliff and he was dead.'

'And you think he committed suicide because of what you said to him?'

'I honestly don't know,' said Alison in a tormented voice. 'From what the police told me he went on to a party after he left me, and he drove away with a girl he'd been living with. Everyone said they seemed quite cheerful, so it might have been an accident, but the uncertainty has haunted me ever since. And the tabloids certainly blamed me for it.'

'How did they get hold of the story?'

Alison sighed.

'The maid overheard us quarrelling and sold exclusive rights to one of the big magazine syndicates. She was sweet on Harley herself, so there was no mention of his violence or drug taking. Only the fact that he had wanted to patch up our marriage and I had refused. I got bags of hate mail from his fans afterwards. Even death threats. That's why I fled to the remotest place I could find, and I've been here ever since.'

'Oh, Alison,' murmured Rod, gripping her shoulders hard. 'So that's what you were trying to hide?'

She looked up at him with a bleak expression and nodded. Then she put into words the fear that had devoured her for years.

'Yes. Oh, Rod, tell me the truth. What do you think? Was it my fault Harley died?'

CHAPTER SEVEN

'OH, MY love,' he said thickly. 'Of course it wasn't! Whether it was suicide or not, Harley's death was self-inflicted, and I can't see that you're in any way to blame for it. Do you really mean to tell me that you've been torturing yourself for years about this?'

She nodded wordlessly. For a long moment she simply stood motionless, feeling too shaken by her confession to speak or move. But incredibly Rod didn't seem to be horrified or repelled by what she had told him. On the contrary, he held her as if she were infinitely fragile and precious.

'Why didn't you tell me before?' he murmured.

'I was afraid that...that you'd be shocked...that you'd blame me!' she blurted out.

His grip tightened reassuringly, and he held her against him as if he would never let her go.

'Don't be a fool!' he said roughly. 'It only makes me more determined than ever to protect you, to try and make you happy. You've got to put all of this behind you, Alison. From here on the past is just a bad dream. Harley's dead now, and I'll make damn sure Quentin never troubles you again.'

His hands were moving, stroking, kneading, exorcising all her tension and fear. She swayed against him with a faint whimper and he suddenly cupped her face in his hands and kissed her. Then kissed her again.

'I wish I didn't have to go away!' he muttered.

Her eyes flew open and she clutched at him, all her

worries about the past suddenly banished by this new catastrophe.

'Go away?' she demanded in a stricken voice. 'Where? Why? You didn't tell me —'

'I came over to tell you tonight and the manager said you were out here. I've got to fly to Sydney tomorrow.'

'Why?'

'I've already stayed in Noosa far too long. I've got other business ventures that I've been neglecting. There's a shopping complex in Parramatta that's crying out for attention and a manufacturing plant... But it would have happened soon anyway. The filming will be finished here in another week, and the whole mob of us will be packing up and leaving then.'

Alison felt a sick sensation, as if she had just plummeted off the edge of a high building. Had time really gone so quickly? But then what had she expected? Somehow she had vaguely thought at the back of her mind that when the film crew packed up and left, Rod would stay on. After all, he had an independent income and a house in Noosa, didn't he?

Now she realised how naïve she had been! Obviously her company had only provided a mild, entertaining interlude until he moved somewhere else. She was so hurt that it was like having a knife piercing her breast. She tried to hide her dismay under a mask of nonchalance.

'Oh, I'm sorry to hear that,' she said coolly, stepping back a pace. 'I'll miss you. We've had some very pleasant outings together.'

He seized her shoulders and thrust his face so close to hers that she could see the bright, angry pinpoints of light in his pupils.

'Don't give me that garbage! I don't want to hear you talk as if we've done nothing more important than drink tea and discuss the weather. What's happening between us is serious, Alison.'

She felt a warm surge of relief, followed by a cold chill of doubt.

'If it's so serious, why are you leaving me?'

Rod let out his breath in a hiss of exasperation.

'I'm not leaving you! I'm not going for ever. It will be a week at most until I get matters straightened out. And, in any case, there's no reason why we have to be parted. I want you to come too.'

Alison's eyes widened in astonishment.

'To Sydney?'

'Yes. And don't look at me as if I've just invited you to the planet Mars.'

She felt as stunned as if he had done. All sorts of conjectures leapt into her mind, but she could only stare at him stupidly, her mouth opening and closing.

'Why do you want me to come to Sydney?' she blurted out at last.

'So that we can keep getting to know each other,' he replied, gazing at her intently. 'And there's another reason too.'

'What other reason?'

'I want you to reconsider auditioning for the role of Charlotte. As you know, we still haven't cast the part, and we'll have to make up our minds quickly now. That part of the film is going to be shot on location in Old Sydney Town, and it won't involve more than two weeks' filming. There are four young women shortlisted for the part, but none of them is a patch on you. If you take the role, it could be the start of a whole new career for you.'

Alison hesitated as a wave of longing swept over her.

'I couldn't possibly,' she said in a tormented voice. 'I couldn't leave Cathy.'

'It's only for a week! I'm sure Lyn would step into the breach and look after her. And if you do decide to pursue a long-term acting career there are other arrangements you can make—a live-in nanny for the times when you have to be away or something like that. There are plenty of fine actresses in the world who are also good mothers.'

A muscle twitched at the corner of Alison's eye.

'People might recognise me,' she protested. 'They might realise who I really am.'

'So what?' demanded Rod, and his voice rose impatiently. 'If you ask me, it would be the best possible thing to come out in the open and get it over! I can see the headline now—HARLEY WINCHESTER'S WIDOW EMERGES FROM FIVE-YEAR SECLUSION.

'All right, there would be gossip and tittle-tattle, but you're strong enough to weather that. And nobody needs to know the things you really want to keep hidden. Like the fact that Harley was a drug addict who was violent and abusive towards you. The focus won't be on him any more, it will be on you and your acting career.

'You've got so much talent, Alison. You ought to put up with the media hype for the sake of doing what you really want to do. Besides, I'll help you fend off the journalists if they get too obstreperous.'

Alison broke free of his hold and paced restlessly around the room. Was Rod right? Should she do it? She hadn't realised just how urgently she wanted to act again until he had dangled this opportunity so temptingly in front of her.

She could do a good job of it, she knew she could! And he was offering to help her, shield her from the media. In any case, she knew that she was more mature now herself, not as vulnerable as she had been five years ago.

Yet there was so much holding her back—not just her panic or her desire for privacy, but more important matters, like Cathy and the need to be the best possible mother to her.

'No, I can't do it! I'm sorry. I'd like to, but I can't.' She searched for an excuse and found a remarkably plausible one. 'I don't want to work with Quentin.'

Rod made a low sound of exasperation in the back of his throat.

'Well, that's fair enough, but there are other directors. If you won't consider doing this film, at least let me introduce you to some other people. Come to Sydney with me for a week, anyway.'

Tingles of alarm ran through Alison's limbs.

'On what basis?' she asked.

'On whatever basis you like! I've got a huge house there and you're more than welcome to stay with me. I won't abuse your trust, Alison. You must know by now how badly I want you, but I'd never take you against your will. Oh, hell! Forget the film directors. Come because of us. Come because I need you.'

'I need you'. The words had such a bittersweet ring to them that Alison felt her resolve crumbling. I need you too, she thought silently. She leaned wistfully into his embrace and then froze.

'What was that?' she demanded.

'What?'

'That creaking sound.'

'Nothing,' Rod assured her impatiently. 'It was just the wind or a floorboard. Old houses creak all the time, but if you're really worried we can go back to my place. It's more comfortable there anyway.'

They locked up the house and walked outside, their arms entwined. Alison was about to climb into her own four-wheel drive when Rod shook his head.

'Don't go off alone. Why don't you come with me? Your vehicle will be safe enough here, and I'll bring you out to get it in the morning before I leave for the airport.'

Alison was silent on the drive back to Noosa, turning over the events of the evening in her mind. To her surprise, now that the ordeal of confessing was over, she felt weak with relief at the final revelation of the secret she had kept hidden so long. Rod didn't blame her or despise her, and he still seemed to care about her. Only now did she realise just how much she had feared his desertion.

For the first time she felt a spark of genuine hope and excitement about the future. It was almost as if his discovery of the tragedy in her past had broken down the last barriers between them. Certainly he had been more outspoken about his feelings for her tonight than ever before the past, despite his disconcerting frankness about his physical attraction to her, he had never revealed much of his deepest emotions or what he intended to do once the filming was over. And she herself had always been too proud and insecure to interrogate him. But now all that seemed to be changing. He wouldn't be inviting her to Sydney or coming back to rejoin her in Noosa if his intentions weren't serious, would he?

For weeks she had been haunted by the fear that he was only amusing himself with her. It had stood like a concrete dam inside her, blocking the impetuous torrent of her own feelings and forcing her to be reserved, cautious, sceptical. But Rod's words tonight seemed to have opened a floodgate inside her, so that the spate of her own emotions was free to burst forth.

Gazing out the window of the car, she felt as if she were being swept along on a giddy tide of longing and hope, passion and exhilaration, yearning and certainty. She no longer felt as if she were on guard, as if she had to protect herself. She was free to be honest, free to ask all she wanted from Rod. So what did she want? Everything, she thought to herself. *Everything*. Passion, love, marriage, another child, a shared life.

She glanced sideways at him as they turned into the road that ran along the river's edge. Catching her gaze, he reached out his left hand and gripped hers.

'Do you need to go home?' he asked.

'N-not really,' she stammered. 'Cathy's sleeping at Lyn's place tonight.'

'Then come to my house. We need some time together.'

Something was singing inside her head, higher and higher, soaring like a bird. It was warm in the car and she wound down the window and let the night air float sluggishly inside. It was charged with an ominous current that lay moist and languorous on her skin. There was something sultry and decidedly sensual about its touch.

'It feels like rain,' said Rod prosaically. 'There'll be a storm before we get home.'

It broke just as they turned into the drive. There was a flash of lightning, a loud rumble of thunder and a sudden tropical downpour. As they dashed from the garage to the front door they were buffeted by rain and enveloped in the heady scent of wet earth and flowers.

'Oh, Lord!' exclaimed Rod as they gained the sanctuary of the hallway. 'I left the French doors to my bedroom balcony open upstairs. The rain will be beating in on the carpet. I'll just go up and close them.'

Brushing the droplets from her hair and eyes, she advanced further into the hall just as his voice echoed down the stairs.

'Come up and join me. I'll get you a towel so that you can dry off.'

With an odd, fluttering sensation in her midriff, she followed him upstairs to the main bedroom. He was just closing the French doors, and she caught a glimpse of rain-blurred darkness and of tree branches thrashing the balcony railing, then Rod lowered the blinds on both doors and turned to face her.

She was intensely conscious of the muted sounds around her—the muffled roar of the storm, the heavy metallic tap of the bronze weights on the blind-cords, the thunder of her own blood beating a wild rhythm through her body. Her senses swam. Dimly she registered that it was a beautiful room, dominated by a vast cane bed and lit by subdued lamps on either side of it. Then Rod crossed the floor and took her in his arms.

That first kiss was electrifying. In the past she had always found his kisses passionate, enticing, achingly sensual. Yet there had always been a sense of some ultimate restraint, as if he were keeping himself under iron control, as if he had vowed not to go too far. This time the control had vanished. He caught her against him with such power that he crushed the breath out of her and she could feel the wild thudding of his heart through his hot, damp shirt.

Her hands slid feebly up his back, touching his straining muscles as she was swept along by his passionate onslaught. Abruptly she too caught fire. As his ravenous, urgent mouth plundered hers she felt her entire body stiffen, as if to launch itself from a high diving tower. Then she plunged. No more misgivings, no more need for guarantees.

An incredible lightness tingled through he and she felt as if she were free falling through dizzying, endless space. Except that the satisfying hardness and heat and urgency of Rod's embrace anchored her to this time, this place, this man. Her lips opened, trembling, to his, and she felt the swift, hot thrust of his tongue and the shudder that went through his muscular frame.

With a faint, whimpering sigh she swayed against him, then clutched at him and kissed him back with a passionate savagery that matched his own. Her blood roared in her ears and she felt fire leap in her groin as Rod hauled her against him, grinding his pelvis into hers. That touch was so brutal and yet so exquisitely sensitive that tremors of heat shimmered through her limbs. Her mouth fluttered free of his and she gasped, looking up at him with a question as old as humanity in her eyes.

'Yes,' he said thickly. 'Yes, sweetheart. It's time that I was deep and hot and hard inside you. I need you, Alison.'

Her whole body was shaking as if she had a fever, throbbing with an intense, tumultuous yearning that could be appeased in only one way. The stormy look in Rod's eyes left her in no doubt that he was suffering the same raging hunger.

With swift, abrupt movements he hauled her flimsy top over her head and flung it away. He took a single harsh breath at the sight of her breasts swelling gently above her lacy bra, then his deft fingers reached behind her back and unfastened the hook, leaving him free to slide the wispy garment off her shoulders. She flinched as he dropped it to the floor, suddenly conscious of her own inadequacies.

Her breasts had never been large, and now that she had borne a child her nipples were no longer pink but a dusky tan. There were other changes too—marks. . . She dropped her head and felt a hot flush of colour burn her cheeks. Rod's fingers tilted her chin.

'Alison?' he said hoarsely. 'What's wrong? You're not frightened of me, are you?'

She shook her head and darted him a quick, embarrassed glance.

'I'm afraid. . .you'll be disappointed in me. That I won't be glamorous enough. . .that my body isn't perfect. . .'

She felt rather than heard his low growl of laughter as he bent his head and nuzzled her hair.

'You precious fool!' he murmured. 'I think you're beautiful exactly as you are.'

Gripping her shoulders, he guided her backwards until the bed bumped her legs and she sat down. With a swift movement Rod fell to his knees in front of her and began to talk softly, telling her how sexy she was. She felt both shocked and enthralled as he told her of his most intimate desires.

As the husky words rose and fell hypnotically his hands moved over her breasts, cupping and caressing them. Then he bent his head and took her nipple into his mouth, sucking with a tantalising skill that sent tremors of pleasure coursing through her entire body. She gasped and arched against him, feeling her nipples tighten into hard, tingling peaks. Without the slightest haste, he transferred his mouth to her other breast and repeated the exquisite torture. Only when she was twisting and moaning under his touch did he rise to his feet and begin undressing.

With a couple of deft movements he kicked off his leather docksider shoes, then pulled his shirt over his head. The movement displayed his ribcage and muscular solar plexus in all their virile power. In the glow of the lamplight his skin gleamed like oiled silk, and Alison felt her breath catch in her throat at the sight of him. It wasn't only his athletic strength and grace that mesmerised her. It was the look on his face.

He did not take his eyes off her as he began unbuckling his leather belt and unzipping his shorts, and the smouldering passion that radiated out from him in waves made her heart thump unsteadily, her breath come in shallow flutters and her whole body pulsate with a hot, intense ache that she had never experienced before.

She wanted him. Wanted him so badly that she felt on fire with urgency. When he paused, and then stripped off his navy blue briefs, she gave a muffled gasp.

He stood for a moment, watching her from under half-closed lids, not attempting to hide his proud, naked arousal. Then he took a step closer, so close that she could feel the heat coming off him in waves, could smell the musky, spicy tang of his masculine scent. Her senses swam at his nearness, and without any conscious choice she reached out and caressed him. He shuddered at her touch and his hand came down on hers.

'Wait,' he muttered hoarsely. 'That might be more than flesh and blood can stand. I want you so badly, Alison, but I want you to be safe. No babies tonight.'

She stretched out on the bed and watched him as he went to the chest of drawers. He was right, of course, and instead of ruining the mood, his decision made her feel loved, protected, cherished. He really cares, she thought gratefully. When he came and lay beside her, and stroked the full length of her flank, she smiled mistily at him.

'One day I'd like nothing better than to be naked inside you,' he whispered. 'But first you have to learn to trust me.'

His hand strayed to the waistband of her skirt. Involuntarily she stiffened .

'Trust me,' he repeated.

With a long sigh she surrendered. To her joy there were no more second thoughts after that. It felt wildly erotic as he slid her skirt and underwear down over her hips, exposing her naked skin to his gaze. And he did plenty of gazing, treating her to a slow, appreciative scrutiny that made her blush.

'I'm going to kiss every inch of you,' he murmured. 'Starting from your feet and working up.'

She had never realised that feet could be so erotic. The moist, teasing brush of his tongue on her soles make her start and giggle. But when his lips began to move up her instep and calf, brushing along the silky inner surface of her thigh, she no longer felt any urge to laugh. Instead a dark heat began to throb deep inside her, and she gasped aloud and clutched at his hair as his kisses reached the most intimate part of her.

'Oh, Rod,' she breathed, half struggling to rise.

'Relax and enjoy it, sweetheart,' he ordered, gently thrusting her back down.

He was totally without shame, and his unfettered delight in her body liberated her in a way she had never experienced before. With Harley it had always been too rough, too quick, and she had sensed a certain disgust beneath his urgency, as if he'd secretly thought the whole business quite repulsive. It had made her feel too embarrassed for enjoyment. But Rod seemed to glory in her responsiveness, teasing and caressing and strok-ing her until she was moist and quivering with need.

Only when she was whimpering and thrusting herself against him did he gather her in his arms, poise himself above her and plunge deep inside her.

She met him with a glad cry, winding her legs around

him and arching her back, revelling in those powerful, pistonlike strokes and the urgency and tenderness with which he held her. The room seemed to spin about her in a sensual kaleidoscope of colours as she opened and closed her eyes, moaning in delight at the touch of his lips and his deep, hard, relentless entry into her innermost being.

She had thought her capacity for pleasure already exhausted, but as he continued to besiege her with such exquisite, maddening skill she found that she was wrong. Her head began to thresh from side to side, her fingers clutched violently at his back, and with a strangled cry she soared into a blissful abandonment which she had never achieved before.

'Alison!'

The word was little more than a distorted groan forced from his lips. His hands clutched at her hair and a deep, shuddering spasm convulsed his body. A moment later he collapsed on top of her, spent and quivering, blindly caressing her face and murmuring her name. Transfigured by joy, she clasped him against her, exulting in the way his heart was pounding and his hot, sweaty body was crushing her into the bed.

'I love you,' she whispered.

Alison was woken the next morning by the raucous squabbling of rainbow lorikeets in the trees outside. For a moment she thought she was in her own bedroom at Noosaville, and lay dreamily watching the tossing shadows of palm trees and bottle brush on the walls. Then something unfamiliar about the bed and the arrangement of furniture alerted her, and she sat up with a stifled gasp. Memory came flooding back and her cheeks burned as she realised she was still naked.

Nor was she the only one. Beside her, sprawled out

luxuriously with one arm flung over her, imprisoning her hips, lay Rod. His masculinity had never been more apparent, and she felt an involuntary thrill of pride and excitement as she gazed down at the tranquil rise and fall of his powerful chest.

She was tempted to trail her fingers over the springy net of dark hair that covered his pectoral muscles, or to kiss the raw outline of his chin, but she refrained. If she did, he would probably haul her into his arms and make violent love to her. The thought filled her with a tingling excitement, but she was content to wait, enjoying a deeper, quieter pleasure. The pleasure of watching him sleep and knowing he was hers.

Suddenly he stirred and muttered in his sleep.

'Marielle!' he said thickly.

Alison froze, feeling as if a bullet had lodged in her heart. She sat up with a violent jerk. The suddenness of her movement must have woken Rod, for he blinked and stared at her. A bemused look spread over his face.

'It is you,' he muttered, shaking his head. 'It really is you. Then we did make love.'

'You thought it was Marielle a moment ago!' exclaimed Alison bitterly, struggling to free herself from the encumbering sheet. She was so hurt and dismayed that all she wanted to do was find a hole to crawl into so that she could sob her heart out in private. Never in her life had she felt such a sense of pain and betrayal. 'I suppose you thought you were making love to her.'

'No!' The word was a raw shout, wrenched from the back of his throat. His powerful hand shot out, gripping her wrist and trapping her. 'No! I didn't think anything of the kind. And I didn't want it either. I just had a bad dream where I was trying to explain to Marielle about what was happening between you and me.'

'Oh, I see!' jeered Alison. 'And what special right has she got to explanations about what's happening between us?'

Rod groaned, and thrust his hair out of his eyes with his free hand.

'None at all!' he said through his teeth.

'And anyway, why did you call it "a bad dream"?' continued Alison in a hurt voice.

'I didn't mean to offend you!' exclaimed Rod in exasperation. 'It was only—'

'Only what?'

'Only that I think we may have jumped into things too hastily,' he growled. 'I'm worried that you may have regrets about it.'

Alison cast him a burning look.

'Is this a sly way of telling me that *you* have regrets about it?'

'I didn't say that!'

'You didn't need to! It's written all over you. You wish we hadn't done it.'

'That's not true. At least. . .'

His words trailed off. And, looking at him for the first time, Alison realised how subdued and evasive his manner was. With an angry cry she wrenched herself free and leapt out of bed. Feeling like a fugitive, she began to gather her scattered clothes, intending to dress and make a run for it. Last night she had been looking forward to spending the rest of her life with Rod. Now she felt as if she never wanted to set eyes on him again.

The brute! The callous, manipulative brute! Obviously all he had wanted was to spend a single night with her and then abandon her. She had only got as far as picking up her tangled underwear when his towering body loomed behind her and he caught her in his arms and spun her round to face him.

'Don't be a fool!' he said roughly.

'I'm not a fool!' she shouted, struggling to free herself. 'I know when I'm being given the brush-off. All you wanted was to go to bed with me and then disappear. It didn't mean anything to you, did it? As far as you're concerned, it was just a one-night stand—and probably a disappointing one at that.'

'Disappointing?' he echoed hoarsely. 'That's ridiculous, Alison. And it wasn't like that at all. You're twisting everything I've said. I just think it was too soon—and it's my fault. I swear I had no intention of making love to you last night, but when I turned around and saw you I couldn't resist. You had that soft glow in your eyes and your lips were half parted. I only meant to kiss you, but instead. . . Well, I should never have rushed you into it like that, but I certainly wasn't doing it as some kind of macho conquest. You're important to me.'

Alison took in an agonised breath and looked up at him warily. In a weird way it made sense, and she wanted to believe him because the alternative was too appalling to contemplate. She didn't want to think that she had given herself to someone who was only exploiting her, who cared nothing for her as a person, but only wanted her as a sex object.

A turmoil of confused emotions warred inside her. Pride, suspicion, yearning, anger. But Rod's intent grey eyes and stern mouth seemed utterly sincere. With a final twinge of misgiving, she allowed herself to be convinced.

'Well, what do we do now?' she asked in a brittle voice.

'If I followed my instincts, I'd tumble you into that bed and make love to you this very minute,' he said, in a voice that sent a tremor of arousal through her. 'But I

think there's something far more important here than
mere instinct. I want you to have time to think about
this relationship, to decide what you really want to do.
As I said, I'm off to Sydney today, and I think it's better
that we don't contact each other while I'm away. I want
you to be sure of your own feelings. When I come back
in a week or so we can talk about it.'

'All right,' whispered Alison reluctantly.

The words almost stuck in her throat, but she forced
them out. She already knew what she wanted. Provided
that Rod returned her feelings, she wanted him as her
life's partner, and she was impatient to have that fact
clearly established. As far as she was concerned, she
would gladly shout it from the rooftops, but Rod's
caution moved her just as much as it grieved her.

He's only doing this because he cares about me, she
thought. It's like the precautions he took last night. He
doesn't want me to suffer from my own impulses.

'That's my girl,' he murmured into her hair, and his
fingers caressed the nape of her neck. Then abruptly he
released her and stepped back a pace. When he spoke
again his voice sounded harsh, and he kept his eyes
averted from her. 'If you could get dressed in the
bathroom, I'd be grateful. I'm not sure that my self-
control will last if I have to watch you naked.'

There was a wry, wistful smile on her lips as she
showered and dressed. Oh, Rod, you romantic, protective idealist! she thought. I'll be glad when this stupid
separation is over and we can be together again. But I
suppose you're right to be careful. We have so much to
consider if we're going to spend our lives together.

He must have used the downstairs bathroom himself,
for he was already shaved and dressed when she
returned to the bedroom. He wore crisp grey trousers, a

pale blue shirt and navy blue loafers, and he was busy packing an expensive-looking suitcase.

'I wish you didn't have to go,' she said with a sigh.

He looked up and smiled briefly at her.

'So do I. But it won't be for long, and you can drive me to the airport if you've got time. Now, come downstairs and we'll console ourselves with breakfast.'

They sat outside under the vine-covered pergola and watched the lazy pelicans and tranquil watercraft as they ate. In spite of her regret at Rod's imminent departure, Alison felt a bittersweet happiness in simply sharing a meal together. The chilled orange juice with its shreds of fruit, the fragrant bacon and fluffy eggs, the muffins and freshly brewed coffee—all had an additional savour simply because of his presence.

I wish we were married, she thought fervently. It would be wonderful to know I could count on his love and passion and companionship every day of my life. I'd like to sit here and listen to him discuss business plans and my acting career, and trips we could make with Cathy, and. . .oh, everything! Everything! I don't think there's any greater happiness than being married to someone you love.

Catching Rod's brooding gaze resting on her, she felt sure that he was thinking the same thing.

'Well, I have to go,' he said at last, looking at his watch and rising to his feet. 'Are you sure it's convenient to drive me to the airport?'

'I'm sure.'

At the airport she was overcome by an urge to cling to him and beg him not to leave.

'Can't I even phone you while you're away?' she asked.

'No,' he replied with mock severity, touching her

cheek with his finger. 'I'll be back in a week and I want you to spend the time thinking.'

Suddenly the boarding announcement crackled over the loudspeaker. Careless of any onlookers, Alison flung herself into Rod's embrace. He hugged her briefly and then detached himself. A strained, slightly aloof expression came over his face.

'Take care of yourself,' he said, not really looking at her. 'And give my love to Cathy.'

She nodded, biting her lip.

'Goodbye,' she whispered.

CHAPTER EIGHT

FOR the next few days Alison obeyed Rod's instructions to think about their relationship. In fact, she thought about nothing else. Yet she did not make a sober, dispassionate analysis of the pros and cons of staying with him, as he would have wanted. Somehow, whenever his image flashed into her mind, it was accompanied by a warm, fuzzy feeling and vague images of orange blossom, wedding marches and choices of honeymoon destinations.

It was only when she went back to work on the film set that she was brought down to earth with a thud.

She had been dreading her next encounter with Quentin, but he seemed either to have forgotten the ugly incident of the previous week or to be completely unfazed by it. His manner when he called Alison into his office on Tuesday morning was blandly matter-of-fact, although she did have the uneasy feeling that there was something very speculative in his gaze as he invited her to sit down.

'I just wanted to tell you that there's a journalist arriving today,' he announced. 'Rod wants you to take her over to Fraser Island tomorrow and show her where we did the filming.'

Alison froze in her seat at the word 'journalist', and then forced herself to relax. If anyone was making a film, it was inevitable that journalists would want to know about it. She was surprised at how steady her voice sounded when she spoke.

'Is someone coming with me to tell her about the filming?'

'No, although she'll be doing an interview with Marielle later on. I gather it's mainly you she wants to talk to.'

'Me?' Alison's composure vanished and the word came out as an unsteady croak. 'Why me?'

Quentin's eyebrows rose at her obvious agitation.

'Well, we told her all about the four-wheel-drive accident, and that's the sort of drama that's bound to pull in readers and viewers. How Rod and I were on the point of death when you came and saved us—that sort of thing. She wants your side of the story too.'

Alison shrank in her chair, hating the idea. At least it wasn't the sort of exposé that she had feared about her relationship with Harley, but still. . .

'I'm not very good at dealing with journalists,' she muttered. 'And quite honestly I don't want to be involved. If we must tell her about the accident, I'd far rather you do it.'

To her surprise, Quentin gave in graciously.

'All right,' he agreed. 'You just drive her around and tell her about the scenery.'

Fortunately the woman who arrived the following day, equipped with a tape recorder and notebook and accompanied by a photographer, seemed perfectly pleasant. All the same, Alison still found it a great ordeal being in their presence. She was conscious of delivering her usual tour guide's spiel in a stilted, unnatural tone and it was only after much persuasion that she allowed herself to be photographed from a distance, with the roaring sea and the bright sun behind her.

She was deeply thankful when it was time to deliver the journalist to Marielle for her interview, and afterwards she drove away from the farmhouse and forgot all about the incident. Then, on Friday morning as she was coming out of the canteen van, Marielle called her over.

'Alison,' she said. 'You must come and see the fax I've just received from that journalist who was here the other day. It's a rough draft of the article she's doing about the filming.'

Alison gave her a strained smile. She still didn't feel comfortable with Marielle, even when she was being nice. Especially when she was being nice.

'Thanks anyway,' she replied, 'but I'm not really interested. It doesn't have much to do with me.'

'Oh, but that's just where you're wrong!' exclaimed Marielle. 'There's such a lot about you in the article. You are a dark horse, aren't you? I had no idea you were keeping so many secrets from us, but Rod has evidently decided that they'll be good publicity for the film.'

Alison felt suddenly paralysed, as if she had been trapped in the path of an oncoming train. The blood drained out of her cheeks and her limbs grew cold. She stared at the actress in horror.

'Are you all right?' asked Marielle. 'You've gone quite pale. You'd better come into my caravan and have a drink. And you might as well read the fax while you're there. There was quite a lot about your acting career in it.'

As if in a nightmare, Alison allowed herself to be led into Marielle's cabin. With trembling hands she picked up the fax and scanned it. It was all there!

Photos of her and Harley in the Rhett Barton film, and even the headline that Rod had suggested— HARLEY WINCHESTER'S WIDOW EMERGES FROM FIVE-YEAR SECLUSION. Worse still, there was the dreadful

truth about Harley's drug addiction and the years of
hell which Alison had endured as his wife. She stared at
the words in horror.

'I can't believe that Rod would allow such stuff to be
printed!' she blurted out.

Marielle looked amused.

'Well, that just shows you, darling—nothing's private.
And you're not the only one whose life is on display.
He's told her all about his relationship with me, and
given her photos of our house in Sydney. I don't mind.
Why should you?'

'What do you mean?' stammered Alison. 'What
relationship? What house in Sydney?'

'Don't you know?' asked Marielle with a ripple of
laughter. 'Well, it's never been any secret. Rod begged
me to marry him years ago, but I didn't think marriage
would suit my freewheeling lifestyle, so we decided to
live together instead. We've got a fabulous house
overlooking Sydney Harbour—look, there's a photo of
us having breakfast together on our back patio. It's a bit
blurred from the fax machine, but you can still see who
it is.'

Alison peered closely at the second sheet of paper
which Marielle was holding out for her to examine, and
her heart sank. Yes, you could see who it was.

'If you and Rod have been living together for so long,
then why didn't you stay with him up here in Noosa?
Why did you go to a hotel?'

Marielle gave her the pitying smile of a woman of the
world.

'Well, we both find we need a little time and space on
our own now and then,' she explained breezily. 'Monog-
amy can be such a bore, can't it? I've always known that
Rod used his holiday home for his little frolics with

other women, but as long he's discreet about it I turn a blind eye. . . Where are you going?'

'Home!' replied Alison in a strangled voice. 'I'm going home. Back to my cabin at Teewah Beach.'

How she got through the next hour, she couldn't remember afterwards. People and conversations seemed to come at her in sickening slow motion, as if she had been in a car accident. At first she was too stunned to feel pain, and she was faintly surprised to hear herself telling Quentin in a matter-of-fact voice that she felt her part in the filming was over and that she would have to leave.

At least none of the other film crew members seemed to be aware of the journalist's article yet, so she was spared the misery of dealing with their curiosity or condolences. Everyone seemed sorry that she was leaving, but their words only buzzed dimly in her ears like a distant swarm of bees.

She seemed to be wrapped in a bubble of shock, which protected her all the way through the drive back to the townhouse and the task of packing and cleaning up. It was only when she went to the school in Tewantin and asked for Cathy to be released from class early that the bubble abruptly burst.

'What's wrong, Mummy?' demanded Cathy as Alison hustled her outside to the minibus. 'We're making cardboard Easter bunnies with fluffy tails. I don't want to go home early. Why do I have to?'

Alison felt a sudden impulse to burst into a storm of weeping. She bit her lip, and suddenly her misery was transformed into anger.

'Because we're moving back to Teewah Beach,' she snapped. 'The party's over. We're going home.'

'What party?' demanded Cathy in bewilderment. 'Mummy, I don't want to go home! I like it here. I want this to be our home, and Rod's bringing me a Puppy Surprise toy from Sydney next week. He promised!'

With an effort Alison managed to keep the tremor out of her voice when she spoke again. After all, this wasn't Cathy's fault, and it was wrong to be cross with her. Miserably she helped her into the minibus, fastened her seat belt and gave her a swift hug.

'I don't think we're going to be seeing Rod any more. The filming's nearly over now.'

'But, Mummy, I like Rod. I want to keep seeing him, and you said we might stay here at Noosa when the filming was finished. You said!'

'Well, things don't always work out the way that grown-ups plan. You'll just have to be a brave girl about it.'

'I don't want to be a brave girl. I hate you, Mummy!' raged Cathy. 'You're mean, mean, mean! I only love Rod.'

As an act of defiance, Cathy groped inside her schoolbag and pulled out the white furry seal which Rod had bought for her at Sea World, hugged it against her and stuck out her lip.

Alison's face crumpled at the sight of the harmless toy. Hastily she slid into her own place behind the wheel and turned her head away, in the hope that Cathy would not see how upset she was. But it was useless. In spite of all her efforts, two hot tears rolled down her cheeks and fell on her faded green beach trousers.

Suddenly Cathy dropped the seal, jumped out of her seat and flung her arms around Alison's neck in a warm, choking hug.

'Don't cry, Mummy!' she pleaded in distress. 'Please don't cry! I'm sorry I was bad.'

Alison held the warm little body against her and fought hard to control her shuddering breaths. It was wrong to frighten Cathy like this! She must deal with her anguish alone.

'You weren't bad, darling,' she assured her. 'You're the best little girl in the whole world and Mummy loves you. I'm sorry about moving back to Teewah Beach, but I'll make it up to you somehow. Now, sit in your seat, because we must get going before the tide comes back in.'

Cathy was very silent on the long drive back along the beach, with the waves thundering on their right hand and the sand flying up around them. Only once did she speak.

'Did you and Rod fight?' she asked bluntly. 'Was he mean to you?'

Alison winced at her daughter's shrewdness.

'Sort of,' she admitted. 'But it doesn't matter. I really don't want to see him any more, Cathy.'

The evening that followed was one of the most miserable of Alison's life. Fortunately Jerry and Lyn had already left for Noosa, so she was spared the ordeal of explanations, and for once Cathy went to bed at eight o'clock without any arguments. Only then did Alison get the chance to sit out on the veranda overlooking the moonlit sea and brood on what had just happened to her.

To say that she was devastated would have been putting it mildly. Even the horror of Harley's addiction, his affairs with other women and his tragic death had never hurt her as deeply as this. It was like some dreadful physical pain ripping her apart. The very intensity of it showed her just how deeply she had fallen in love with Rod.

Even now she could scarcely bring herself to believe that she had been so utterly wrong in her judgement of his character. All right, he might be high-handed, scheming, secretive, but she would never have believed he could be so blatantly callous and dishonest!

How could he have held her so tenderly and promised to come back to her when all the time he was planning to desert her? And why, why had he taken such trouble to win Cathy's affection as well as her own? How could he have been so cruel? A sudden sense of rebellion rose in her and she paced distractedly across the veranda.

'I can't believe it, I won't believe it,' she muttered to herself. 'Rod couldn't be so heartless!'

But what else was she to believe? All the evidence was there in black and white, wasn't it? Rod was the only person apart from Lyn and Jerry who knew the truth about Harley's death, and torture wouldn't have dragged it past their lips! No, it must have been Rod who had betrayed her trust. And that wasn't the worst betrayal either, not by a long way.

The worst betrayal was the sickening discovery that he had been involved with Marielle all along and had never intended his relationship with Alison to be anything more than a fleeting affair. No wonder he had told her not to phone him and hadn't given her a forwarding address in Sydney. What a gullible fool he must think her! She buried her face in her hands and groaned aloud.

It was after midnight when she went to bed, her eyes swollen and red, her throat sore and her head aching. She had expected to lie awake tossing and turning, but sheer exhaustion made her slip into a deep sleep.

The sun was flooding brightly through the flimsy curtains of her bedroom when she finally stirred, blinked and looked at her bedside clock.

'Oh, no! It's after eight o'clock!' she exclaimed. 'Cathy will be wanting her breakfast.'

Yet when she padded into the living-room in her bare feet, the rest of the cabin seemed strangely quiet. There was no ginger-haired child singing to herself as she cut out paper dolls or carefully set the breakfast table. And Cathy didn't usually go outside until Alison herself was up. Well, perhaps she had overslept too. . .

Quietly Alison turned the knob of her daughter's bedroom door, peeked in, but there was no sign of Cathy. Feeling the first prickle of alarm, she hurried across to the front door and opened it wide.

'Cathy!' she shouted, standing on the veranda and cupping her hands around her mouth.

Silence.

'Cathy!' she shouted again.

This time the lack of response sent a sickening jolt of panic through her. Heedless of her nightdress and bare feet, she ran down the steps and across to Jerry and Lyn's cabin. Pulling open the unlocked front door, she burst inside.

'Cathy, if you're hiding, come out at once! Answer me!'

Still no answer.

By now her fear was like a lump of lead in the pit of her stomach. Could Cathy have gone down to the beach alone? But she never did that! All the same. . .

Alison set off at an anxious trot, stumbling and swearing as her feet sank into the wheel ruts left in the sand by her four-wheel drive the previous night. But when she shaded her eyes against the glare and scanned the vast expanse of beach it was as empty and desolate as ever.

There must be some explanation. There must. She must be hiding or something.

Thoroughly agitated and gasping for breath, Alison pounded back up the steep slope and burst into her own cabin. Wrenching open Cathy's bedroom door, she looked in every possible hiding place—under the bed, in the wardrobe, in the angle between the chest of drawers and the wall. Then she saw the note.

It was a white square of paper half hidden by the rumpled nest of blankets and sheets on Cathy's bed. As Alison read it her blood ran cold.

> Dear Mummy
> I think you only came back here becos you kworeld with Rod. I dont like you to be sad so I am going to Rods howse to make him say sorry for being mean to you.
>
> Love
> Cathy

A sickening rush of dizziness threatened to make her fall to the floor in a dead faint. Instead she sat down heavily on Cathy's bed, dropped her head between her knees and shuddered. In a moment the faintness passed, to be replaced by a sense of horror and guilt that was so overwhelming she felt as if she were on the verge of hysteria. Her hands shook as she lifted the note again and reread it.

'I must stay calm, I must stay calm,' she said aloud, springing to her feet and pacing around the room in her agitation. 'She can't have gone far; I'm bound to find her in the next few minutes.'

Terrifying images swept into her mind of all the dangers her daughter might have to face. Packs of wild dingoes like those which had frightened Alison on Fraser Island, huge goannas with long reptilian claws that could slash a child's abdomen open, poisonous snakes, sunstroke, drowning.

I must stop this, she thought, trying to rein in her agonised imagination. I must think and plan calmly. Oh, if only Rod were here! The thought sprang unbidden to her mind and brought with it a rush of longing for his coolness, his rocklike reliability in moments of crisis, his power to organise and control. And then she realised that there was a chance that Rod was back from Sydney by now, that he had probably arrived in Noosa the previous evening.

Without even pausing to think, she ran into the other room, snatched up the radio phone and called his number.

'Come on, come on!' she urged frantically as the number rang and rang.

Then suddenly Rod's voice came down the line, deep, vibrant, unbelievably reassuring.

'Hello? Rod Swift here.'

'Rod! It's Alison.'

'Alison! What are you—?'

'Rod, I'm out at Teewah Beach at the cabin, and the most terrible thing has happened. Cathy has run away.'

'What? Why? When? Are you sure?'

She took a deep breath and tried to organise her thoughts.

'Yes, I'm sure. She thought you and I had quarrelled and she was heading for your house. I don't know when she left. Some time between midnight last night and about eight o'clock this morning. Oh, Rod, I'm so worried about her!' Her voice broke.

'Alison, stay calm,' he ordered. 'She can't have got very far on foot. Have you been out to look for her? And have you checked both cabins thoroughly?'

'Yes, yes,' replied Alison distractedly. 'I've searched all around the area near here and there's no sign of her. Jerry and Lyn have gone to Noosa and there's no one to help me.' Suddenly, without warning, tears began to stream down her face. 'Rod, you've got to come! I need you.'

His voice was stern and yet surprisingly comforting.

'Alison, you must stay calm for Cathy's sake. Don't worry, I'll organise a search party from this end and I'll come out to join you as soon as I possibly can. In the meantime what I want you to do is this. Can Cathy read?'

'Yes. Only simple stuff, but I don't see—'

'Good. Then write out a simple sign in block capitals and tape it to the front door of your cabin telling her to stay there if she comes back. Leave a teddy or something with it—something reassuring—and take one of your four-wheel-drive vehicles out and search for her along the beach. If you haven't found her within an hour, come back to the cabin and wait there. Have you got that?'

'Y-yes,' stammered Alison.

'Good. Then I'll be with you as soon as I can.'

Feeling drained of all emotion except sheer terror, Alison set down the radio phone and hurried to obey Rod's instructions. She found a large sheet of cardboard and printed a message on it in red text.

> DEAR CATHY,
> I HAVE GONE TO LOOK FOR YOU. IF YOU COME BACK, STAY HERE AT THE CABIN AND WAIT FOR ME. I'LL BE HOME SOON.
> I LOVE YOU,
> MUMMY.

Her tears threatened to spill over again, but she dashed them away and taped the notice to the front door of the cabin. Following Rod's suggestion, she went to look for a soft toy to leave behind for added reassurance. Perhaps that white seal that he had bought for her at Sea World. . .

But when she searched Cathy's bedroom she found that Cathy had taken the seal with her. That sent a strange little pang through her—a pang of regret and something close to jealousy. In spite of all the evidence, she hadn't realised how deeply attached Cathy had become to Rod. Well, there was no point dwelling on all that now. She must get out and find her daughter before it was too late.

She drove slowly and steadily along the sands, anxiously scanning the blinding brightness for any sign of a small, trudging figure. But after she had covered about ten miles, she was forced to turn back with a chill feeling in her stomach.

Surely Cathy couldn't have walked further than that? Then where was she? Had she gone into the sea to cool off and been swept out by the treacherous currents and drowned? Had she struck inland, hoping to find a short cut, and become lost in the dense bushland there? Or had she already sneaked back home, undetected by her mother?

Comforted by this thought, Alison headed back towards the cabin. She had almost reached the turn-off when she heard a roaring noise in the air overhead, and, to her surprise and relief, a helicopter landed on the firm sand about a hundred metres in front of her. Stopping her vehicle, she jumped out and ran towards it. As she did so a familiar figure ducked low to avoid the sweeping rotors and ran to meet her.

'Rod!' she gasped as he caught her in his arms and hugged her fiercely. 'Oh, Rod, I'm so glad you're here!'

'Have you found her?' he demanded.

She shook her head.

'No, I'm hoping she might be back in the cabin by now. Come up with me and look.'

They both climbed into the four-wheel drive and jolted up the hill to the cabin. But the notice on the front door and the old one-eyed teddy remained undisturbed, and a second thorough search revealed no sign of Cathy. Alison caught her breath on a dry sob.

'Don't, don't, my darling,' urged Rod, hauling her against him and hugging her hard. 'You mustn't panic, we'll find her.'

'But the dingoes,' she said incoherently. 'She'll get lost. Goannas. . . What if. . .? Oh, Rod, it's all my fault!'

'Now, now,' he said bracingly, scrubbing her face with a clean white handkerchief and hushing her as if she were a frightened child. 'She can't have gone very far, and at least it's very simple to find the way. All she has to do is keep the sea on her left hand and the sand cliffs on her right and eventually she'll arrive at the turn-off for the Noosa ferry.'

'I know,' moaned Alison. 'But she's only six years old. What about the tides? What if she goes inland? How on earth are we going to find her?'

Rod became brisk and practical.

'Sit down,' he ordered. 'And I'll make you some hot tea with lots of sugar in it. I've already organised a massive search operation. I've notified the police and I've got a huge group of volunteers ready to look for her. I've also asked your brother and sister-in-law to come here and stay with you, and I've hired a helicopter myself so that I can search the area by air.'

'Oh, Rod,' breathed Alison. 'I don't know what I'd do without you.'

Her hatred for him now seemed remote and far away, submerged by her gratitude and the need to co-operate in something of far more importance. As Rod set down a mug of heavily sugared tea in front of her Alison gave him a feeble smile.

'Thanks,' she muttered.

It wasn't long before the action really heated up. A second helicopter arrived with the Search and Rescue team, and her brother and sister-in-law drove up shortly afterwards. They were all equipped with maps, and the room began to take on the atmosphere of a commando headquarters.

'I'll be off in my helicopter,' said Rod.

'Can't I come with you?' begged Alison.

'Don't you want to stay here in case she finds her own way back?'

'I don't think I could bear the waiting,' she admitted frankly. 'I'd rather feel as if I were doing something, and if you're concentrating on flying you'll need someone to look around. Anyway, I'm sure Lyn would be prepared to stay here and radio us immediately if she turns up.'

'Of course I will,' agreed Lyn.

It was the most harrowing experience of Alison's life. All through the day they searched, until her head was throbbing from the glaring sunlight and the sweat was pouring off her. By nightfall she was frantic, and only the need to keep doing something allowed her to stand by a hot water urn with Lyn dispensing coffee and sandwiches and fruit. Everyone was kind to her, but it was only to Rod that she could admit her deepest fears.

As a new group of volunteers went out into the night, with four-wheel drives and torches, she blurted out her feelings to him.

'I can't bear to think of her being alone and frightened, spending the night out in the open. What on earth will become of her?'

Rod gripped her shoulder comfortingly.

'Don't worry too much. It's not cold, there's plenty of drinking water in the creeks and she'll probably eat shellfish if she gets hungry.'

Alison was silent, torturing herself with images of the hazards outside.

'You must go to bed and get some rest,' insisted Rod, turning her in the direction of her bedroom.

'No,' she cried. 'It feels wrong to go to sleep when she's in danger.'

'Well, I won't take you out in the helicopter tomorrow if you don't,' he threatened. 'I promise I'll wake you up the instant we hear anything tonight. Now, here's a mild sedative that the Search and Rescue doctor has prescribed for you. I want you to take it— that's an order.'

She opened her mouth to argue, but the strained look in Rod's eyes showed her that he was suffering too. Not as much as she was, but there was no question that he was distressed. As their eyes met she felt a bond of silent sympathy and support, as if they were both parents sharing an unendurable strain.

'We'll find her, Alison, we'll find her,' he vowed, hugging her hard.

Throughout the heartbreaking day that followed, she began to think that he was wrong. There was the same monotonously brilliant sky, roaring sea and empty sand.

By now they had scoured every mile of beach between the cabin and the ferry turn-off without success. Yet there was still a chance that Cathy had gone inland. In most places the sand cliffs were far too rugged for a six-year-old to climb, but there were several spots, especially near creek mouths, where the slope was gentler.

It was in these areas that Rod concentrated his aerial

search, but by nightfall on the second day there was still no result. A fresh shift of volunteers continued by torchlight throughout the night, and on Monday morning Rod and Alison went out again in the helicopter.

By now Alison felt like a zombie. The whole experience had taken on a blurred, nightmare quality. If it had not been for Rod, she would have lost her control completely, but somehow he was keeping her sane, feeding her hope, allowing her to function. She was staring down at another patch of hateful, featureless, grey-green bushland, when Rod suddenly gave a shout.

'What's that down there between the trees? Something bright pink!'

Alison was instantly alert, her gaze following his pointing finger.

'Cathy has a pink schoolbag,' she gasped. 'Oh, Rod, do you think it's her?'

'I can't see with all these damned trees. Wait, and I'll go as close as I can.'

He went so low that the tops of the trees flailed violently in the downdraft. Then suddenly, to Alison's horror, he turned the helicopter away.

'Where are you going?' she shrieked. 'That's the wrong way!'

'We can't land there. We'll have to go down to the beach and walk back up. I'll drop a marker nearby so that we can find the spot again.'

It was the longest fifteen minutes of Alison's life as they left the helicopter, raced up the bank of the creek and plunged into the dense bushland. Shrubs scratched at their arms and legs, the sun beat down pitilessly and the air was hot and pungent with the scent of eucalyptus.

'Cathy!' she shouted.

There was no sound except for the shrilling of cicadas

and the distant gurgle of the creek. Suddenly Rod let out a whoop and pointed. Scanning the grey-green foliage, Alison caught a glimpse of something pink through the bushes ahead. Rod darted forward and picked up the abandoned object.

'It's her schoolbag. It's got her name on it.'

'Well, where is she?'

And then she saw her. Curled up in the shadow of a bush, lying ominously still. Rod got to her first and felt for the pulse in her throat. Alison's heart gave a terrifying lurch.

'She's not—?'

'No. Her heartbeat's fine. It's just exhaustion, I think.'

In an instant Alison was beside him, taking in every detail of the scratched arms and legs, the dirty, tear-stained face and the toy seal still clutched in Cathy's arms. With an anguished cry of relief she hugged her sleeping daughter violently against her.

Cathy twitched and sat up. The momentary despair in her eyes was replaced by a sudden, incredulous joy.

'Mummy!' she cried.

CHAPTER NINE

IT WAS another twenty-four hours before Alison let Cathy out of her sight. The doctor on duty admitted her to Nambour Hospital for observation, and Alison was allowed to sleep in the bed beside her in the children's ward.

The following morning Rod came to visit them both in hospital. Cathy was sitting up, eating cereal and chattering happily. Apart from a sunburnt face, half a dozen mosquito bites and several scratches covered by sticking plaster, she was her usual boisterous self.

'Then I banged the pipi shells on the rocks and poked them out with a stick and ate them. And I—'

She stopped at the sight of Rod and beamed, brandishing her toy seal.

'Hello, Rod. Thank you for rescuing me. Do you know Sealy and I are going to be on television tonight?'

Rod gave a mock scowl.

'Well, I hope you tell other children what a naughty thing it is to run away,' he warned. 'You scared the life out of us.'

Cathy shrank down below the covers and looked repentant.

'I know. I'm sorry, I won't do it again. Wow, is that for me?'

Rod tossed a toy puppy onto the bed beside the seal and nodded.

'And these are for your mother,' he added, producing a magnificent sheaf of clove-scented red carnations from behind his back.

Alison gasped and stammered something incoherent as he pressed them into her hands.

'Did you bring those to tell Mummy you were sorry?' asked Cathy with interest.

Rod looked baffled.

'Sorry for what?'

'Mummy said you were mean to her. That's why she moved back to Teewah, and she cried and cried in her room, so I ran away to find you and make you say sorry.'

'Did you, now?' murmured Rod thoughtfully. 'You know, Cathy, I think your mother and I need to have a long talk. May I borrow her for a while?'

'You can have her all day if you like,' agreed Cathy generously. 'But you will come back tonight, won't you, Mummy?'

Alison felt a sudden surge of despair. Up until that moment she had been so preoccupied with the joy of finding Cathy that she had pushed the problem of Rod to the back of her mind. Now, with Rod frowning at her across the hospital bed, the awkwardness of her position struck her anew.

She still felt hurt and outraged by his treachery, but there was no denying he had saved her precious daughter's life. If he wanted a private explanation of why she had left him, she would have to give it to him— however painful she found it. It certainly wasn't the kind of thing she could discuss here in the children's ward.

'All right,' she muttered. 'I'll be back as soon as I can, Cathy.'

She had a few words with the doctor on duty and left the hospital.

'Whatever this is about,' said Rod calmly as he opened the car door for her, 'we're going to wait until we get home to discuss it. You look just about all in, Alison, and I don't want you breaking down from the strain of what you've been through.'

'Then why did you put me through it?' she flared.

Rod shook his head with a baffled expression, but said nothing. Only when they were safely inside his living-room with cold drinks in front of them did he finally speak.

'Now, what's this all about?' he asked, laying his hand on Alison's knee. 'If I did something "mean" to you, I'm genuinely sorry, but I must admit I'm completely mystified as to what I've done.'

'Mystified!' retorted Alison with a short laugh. 'So you have a completely clear conscience about that journalist's article, do you?'

'What on earth are you talking about?'

'You know very well what I'm talking about! Although I don't suppose it occurred to you that the journalist would fax a rough draft of the article to Marielle before she published it.'

'Are you talking about that woman who came out to Fraser Island to write a story about the film for one of the women's magazines?'

'Yes, I am!' hissed Alison. 'And what a story you gave her! All that stuff about Harley and me was in there. You're the only one who knew it apart from Lyn and Jerry—and they would never have revealed it.'

Rod's face darkened.

'And you think I would?' he demanded. 'What the hell kind of opinion do you have of me, Alison? I would have walked on live coals before I did such a thing.'

'Then who did? Nobody else knew about it except Lyn and Jerry.'

Rod snapped his fingers as a look of comprehension blazed in his eyes.

'Quentin!' he growled. 'That night he made advances to you at the farmhouse at Eumundi we were talking about it then. After I booted him out he could easily have come back and overheard us, and he's spiteful enough to have spilt the beans.'

Alison was silent, juggling her thoughts. Yes, it was possible. Probable, even.

'Well, that's not the worst thing!' she burst out. 'The worst thing is all the stuff about you and Marielle in the article.'

Rod looked perplexed again.

'What stuff?'

'About how you've been living together in a house in Sydney for years. There were photos too, and Marielle told me all about it.'

'That callous, lying mischief-maker! Now I know who's behind all this. Quentin may have made the bullets, but Marielle is the one who fired them. When is this article due out?'

Alison winced at the ferocity of his tone.

'I don't know,' she admitted.

'Well, I'll have it stopped,' he vowed, springing to his feet. 'I'll threaten Marielle with court action if she spreads any more lies about me. Just wait here.'

He strode into his study and she heard the sound of raised voices over the telephone line. At last Rod slammed down the receiver and came back, still looking white with rage.

'What's going on?' demanded Alison.

He sank into a chair, poured himself a drink and then pushed the jug of juice towards Alison.

'I've never felt so much like strangling someone in my life!' he exclaimed. 'But don't worry, it's all under control. The article won't appear in print and you'll get a written apology from Marielle for her lies.'

'Lies?' echoed Alison. 'Do you mean you don't live with her, then?'

'No!' he snarled. 'I haven't lived with her for eight years.'

'But you did once?'

'Yes. Fool that I was! When I was twenty-seven years old I was convinced that I was in love with Marielle and I proposed to her. She wasn't keen on the idea of marriage, and she suggested that we should live with each other instead. After a few months it became clear that it was a complete mistake for both of us, and I moved out again.

'I told her to keep the house, which I had bought and put in our joint names, so technically speaking I suppose it's true that we share a house, but I've never spent a night in it since we split up. The most I've ever done is to have an occasional meal there, always in the company of other people. Marielle and I have never renewed our love affair.'

'Then why did she lie to me?'

'I think she's the original dog in the manger,' replied Rod in exasperation. 'She didn't want to marry me herself, but she didn't want anyone else to do so either. It's as if she thinks she still has some rights over me—which is crazy when you consider how she flits from affair to affair herself. She's sleeping with Quentin at the moment, you know.'

Alison blinked.

'And she still thinks she can have you on a string too? But that's ridiculous!'

'I suppose it's my fault, really. After we broke up I agreed to her request that we should remain on friendly terms, and I occasionally escorted her to first night parties at the theatre and that sort of thing. That was all there was to it, I swear it. Of course, the Press has made more of it from time to time—no doubt with Marielle's encouragement. I could have made a fuss, but it never really mattered to me until now.'

'So why is it different now?' asked Alison.

Rod reached out and gripped her hand.

'I think you know the answer to that,' he said. 'The reason it's different is that I've fallen in love with you.'

'I've fallen in love with you'. Her heart sang at the words.

'Do you really mean that?' she asked.

'Yes, I mean it,' he insisted.

'There's so much I don't understand about you!' she burst out. 'For a long time I was afraid that you were a playboy—that you were the kind of man who would always avoid commitments. But now it seems that's not true.'

Rod pulled a wry face.

'It's not true now, but in some ways that's not a bad description of the way I used to be. For many years I was afraid of commitment.'

'Why?'

'Oh, it goes back to my youth. I had a very close, loving relationship with my mother, but she died of cancer when I was fourteen. My father replaced her three months later by marrying his mistress. That lasted about two years, until he found someone else. It made me so bitter and cynical about relationships that I was afraid to get too deeply involved myself—afraid that I would either love someone and lose her, or that I'd turn out to be the same kind of cynical, callous bastard as my father.'

'But you can't have gone for years without any involvement,' protested Alison.

'No, there were involvements—if you could call them that. But only ever with women who were as hard as nails and not likely to be hurt when it ended. I made sure of that.'

'Then where did Marielle come into it?' asked Alison.

Rod gave a mirthless laugh.

'I made the mistake that so many people do of assuming that what you see on the cinema screen is reality. When I was twenty-seven years old I saw Marielle in a film about a woman whose husband was wrongly arrested for spying in World War One. I was shaken to the core by her portrayal of love and grief, her concern for her husband and her commitment to her children.

'What I didn't realise was that with Marielle it's only acting—there's no substance underneath. I asked a mutual friend to arrange an introduction and the rest is history. It didn't take me long to discover that she was totally incapable of commitment in real life.'

'Is that why you went off mountaineering in the Swiss Alps and diving in Vanuatu and all those strange things?' asked Alison.

'Yes. The end of the affair left a pretty sour taste in my mouth. Combined with my cynicism about my father, it made me convinced that any hopes I had of a happy marriage were just pure moonshine. And then something happened to change my outlook.'

'What was that?'

A nostalgic look came into Rod's eyes.

'Living with some villagers in Vanuatu,' he replied. 'I'd like to take you there some time, Alison. The people live in complete poverty by our standards, and there's still malaria in some districts, but they seem to be extraordinarily happy. And it's quite obvious that the source of their happiness is their relationships with each other. There's so much love and warmth and family feeling among them.

'Eventually I realised that I would be a complete fool if I allowed Marielle to embitter me for life. When I finally moved back to Australia I knew exactly what I wanted, but I didn't know if I'd ever find it until I met you.'

'What do you mean?'

'Well, when we first met I was immediately attracted to you, and intrigued by the aura of tension that seemed to surround you. You were like some startled wild creature and I wanted to find out what had made you that way. But the moment when you really stunned me was when you acted out that scene from the Eliza Fraser movie.

'It was electrifying. I could feel the hairs rising on the back of my neck and I was totally convinced of your terror and courage and your passionate devotion to your husband. There was only one question in my mind. Were you capable of such intense emotions in real life, or were you another woman like Marielle? Able to project it all on screen, but incapable of any deep feeling in real life.

'I didn't know, but I was determined to find out. Then, before I could really start probing, that dingo pack arrived and surrounded you.'

Alison shuddered at the memory.

'I was terrified,' she admitted candidly. 'It was such a relief when you arrived and chased them off, but then you kissed me and that was even more terrifying.'

Rod put his other hand on hers.

'It was for me too,' he agreed. 'Because I didn't only feel the normal impulse I would have felt to help anyone in danger. What I felt was a really fierce, instinctive urge to shield you, to protect you. I felt as if you were my woman. When I kissed you I knew that what was happening was serious, but you were so shy and skittish—like some wild creature ready to vanish.

'Maybe I should have just let you run for cover, but I didn't believe you were genuinely happy with the life you had chosen. So I made a vow that I was going to coax you out of it, although I knew I'd have to go carefully for fear of startling you.'

'If you were going so carefully, why did you kiss me that day when I went swimming at your house?'

Rod's eyes suddenly lit with mischief.

'Because I couldn't resist you,' he said. 'But it was bad luck that Marielle turned up when she did.'

'I thought she was having an affair with you.'

'That's exactly what she wanted you to think, damn her. After I took you home I knew I'd lost ground with you, and I didn't know if you'd ever agree to go out with me again.'

'I probably wouldn't have done if you hadn't been so sneaky about inviting me to Sea World with Cathy. She made certain I couldn't refuse.'

Rod grinned.

'That little bombshell has been quite a useful ally, on the whole,' he said appreciatively. 'Not only that, but I've grown genuinely fond of her. When that woman at Sea World thought I was her father, that really stirred me. It was becoming quite clear to me that that was exactly what I wanted. For the three of us to be a family and maybe even to have more children, if you were willing.'

'You scared the life out of me when you told me that at dinner, barely a week after I'd met you.'

Rod sighed.

'I knew I was moving too fast for you, but I could see so clearly what I wanted. I tried to backpedal and take it more slowly, to give you a chance to get to know me better, then after you told me the truth about Harley's death I lost my head. I didn't intend to make love to you that night, but I was carried away by my own feelings for you. I wanted to show you how much I cared about you.'

Alison's mouth contorted.

'It seemed a rather odd way to go about it when you gave me the brush-off the following morning!'

'That's not true!' protested Rod. 'It was just that I felt terribly guilty when I woke up the next day. I was afraid I'd taken advantage of you while you were still in a highly emotional state. I wanted you to be sure of your feelings for me, not to be under any kind of pressure.'

'I thought you were having second thoughts because you were still involved with Marielle—especially when you called out her name in your sleep.'

Rod winced.

'Poor Alison! I'm sorry about that. I know I had some confused dream about telling Marielle that I loved you and I never wanted to see her again, but I don't honestly remember what it was all about. I do know that I was afraid I had taken advantage of you, that I wanted you to have time to think, to reconsider. Instead of which she seems to have conned you into believing that I was only exploiting you.'

Alison gave a long, shuddering sigh.

'That really hurt,' she agreed. 'Far worse than all the misery with Harley—because I was genuinely in love with you, Rod, and I couldn't bear to think you'd do that to me. Cathy took it to heart too.'

'It still gives me the cold horrors to think that she ran away because of it. And if it was bad for me, it must have been a thousand times worse for you. I couldn't bear to think of you suffering like that. I would have ripped apart every shrub in Queensland with my bare hands to find her.'

'Well, you did,' whispered Alison. 'And I'll be grateful to you for the rest of my life.'

Rod's hands travelled up and gripped her shoulders.

'I don't want only your gratitude, Alison,' he said urgently. 'I want you to marry me. Will you?'

Alison looked back at him with her eyes shining.

'Oh, Rod,' she murmured with a long, shaky sigh. 'I thought you'd never ask. Of course I will.'

His grip tightened so fiercely that she almost cried out at the pressure of his fingers digging into her flesh.

'Do you really feel the same way towards me as I do to you?' he demanded.

'Yes, I do.'

'Then say it. For heaven's sake, say it! Put me out of my misery. Tell me, so I'll know it's true.'

'I love you, Rod,' she said haltingly, still self-conscious about using the words.

He dragged her into a crushing embrace.

'You're sure? You're absolutely sure?'

'Yes,' she murmured, winding her arms around his neck and lifting her parted lips to his. 'Yes. Yes. Yes! I always was sure of my feelings. It was only yours that had me worried.'

'Well, don't ever worry again,' he growled. 'Because I love you with all my heart, Alison. And I intend to love you more with every passing day. I want to wed you and bed you and give you children and spend the rest of my life with you. Will that do?'

Abruptly he rose to his feet and lifted her bodily off the couch. A quiver of expectant excitement tingled through her limbs as he took the stairs in long, urgent strides. She was in no doubt at all as to their destination. Sure enough, he stopped on the threshold of the bedroom and gazed down at her with a smouldering hunger that made her pulses leap.

'Well?' he prompted.

She clasped her arms more firmly around his neck and gave a sigh of total surrender.

'That will do beautifully,' she said.

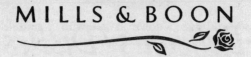

MILLS & BOON

Next Month's Romances

Each month you can choose from a wide variety of romance with Mills & Boon. Below are the new titles to look out for next month.

Available from WH Smith, John Menzies, Volume One, Forbuoys, Martins, Woolworths, Tesco, Asda, Safeway and other paperback stockists.

Delicious Dishes

Would you like to win a year's supply of simply irresistible romances? Well, you can and they're FREE! Simply match the dish to its country of origin and send your answers to us by 31st December 1996. The first 5 correct entries picked after the closing date will win a year's supply of Temptation novels (four books every month—worth over £100). What could be easier?

A	LASAGNE		GERMANY
B	KORMA		GREECE
C	SUSHI		FRANCE
D	BACLAVA		ENGLAND
E	PAELLA		MEXICO
F	HAGGIS		INDIA
G	SHEPHERD'S PIE		SPAIN
H	COQ AU VIN		SCOTLAND
I	SAUERKRAUT		JAPAN
J	TACOS		ITALY

Please turn over for details of how to enter ☞

How to enter

Listed in the left hand column overleaf are the names of ten delicious dishes and in the right hand column the country of origin of each dish. All you have to do is match each dish to the correct country and place the corresponding letter in the box provided.

When you have matched all the dishes to the countries, don't forget to fill in your name and address in the space provided and pop this page into an envelope (you don't need a stamp) and post it today! Hurry—competition ends 31st December 1996.

Mills & Boon Delicious Dishes
FREEPOST
Croydon
Surrey
CR9 3WZ

Are you a Reader Service Subscriber? Yes ❑   No ❑

Ms/Mrs/Miss/Mr _____

Address _____

_____

_____ Postcode _____

One application per household.

You may be mailed with other offers from other reputable companies as a result of this application. If you would prefer not to receive such offers, please tick box.   ❑

C396
F